'Of course there's something in it for me. I need this deal finalised. So I'll replace Tom and help you prune. And when the pruning's done and dusted—to your satisfaction, of course—then you will sign the contract.'

'But—'

'No. *You're* the one who made it clear you'd never do business with a Chatsfield, and that anyone with the Chatsfield name should be tarred with the same brush. I'd like the opportunity to show you that you can't just write us all off that way. I'd like the opportunity to prove that you can do business with a Chatsfield and not regret it.'

'Six weeks,' she snapped. 'At least.'

That long? There was a moment's hesitation before he nodded. 'Six weeks will be perfect. And if there are any scandals involving my family—any at all in that time—then you can choose to walk away from the deal. Otherwise, at the end of six weeks, you sign the contract and the deal between Chatsfield and Purman Wines is done. Do we have a deal?'

Holly couldn't say anything. Not right now. She was too busy working out how she'd lost an advantage that had seemed to her, such a very short time ago, unassailable.

She'd had the high moral ground. But the rock-solid ground she'd been so sure of had turned to quicksand. She'd been moments away from being rid of this man with the cool grey eyes and the too-big feet, moments from freedom, and suddenly events had overtaken her and the goalposts had shifted.

Because Franco was staying and certainty had departed.

It was supposed to be the other way around.

Step into the opulent glory of the world's most elite hotel,
where clients are the impossibly rich
and exceptionally famous.

Whether you're in America, Australia, Europe or Dubai,
our doors will always be open...

Welcome to

The Chatsfield

Synonymous with style, sensation... and scandal!

For years, the children of Gene Chatsfield—
global hotel entrepreneur—have shocked the world's media
with their exploits. But no longer! When Gene appoints a
new CEO, Christos Giatrakos, to bring his children into
line, little does he know what he's starting.

Christos's first command scatters the Chatsfields
to the furthest reaches of their international holdings—
from Las Vegas to Monte Carlo, Sydney to San Francisco...
But will they rise to the challenge set by a man
who hides dark secrets in his past?

Let the games begin!

Your room has been reserved, so check in to enjoy
all the passion and scandal we have to offer.

Ref: 00106875

www.thechatsfield.com

The Chatsfield

SHEIKH'S SCANDAL, Lucy Monroe
PLAYBOY'S LESSON, Melanie Milburne
SOCIALITE'S GAMBLE, Michelle Conder
BILLIONAIRE'S SECRET, Chantelle Shaw
TYCOON'S TEMPTATION, Trish Morey
RIVAL'S CHALLENGE, Abby Green
REBEL'S BARGAIN, Annie West
HEIRESS'S DEFENCE, Lynn Raye Harris

8 volumes to collect—you won't want to miss out!

TYCOON'S TEMPTATION

BY
TRISH MOREY

First published in Great Britain 2014
by Mills & Boon, an imprint of Harlequin (UK) Limited,
Eton House, 18-24 Paradise Road, Richmond, Surrey, TW9 1SR

© 2014 Harlequin Books S.A.

Special thanks and acknowledgement are given to Trish Morey
for her contribution to *The Chatsfield* series.

ISBN: 978-0-263-24293-5

Trish Morey is an Australian who's also spent time living and working in New Zealand and England. Now she's settled with her husband and four young daughters in a special part of South Australia, surrounded by orchards and bushland and visited by the occasional koala and kangaroo. With a lifelong love of reading, she penned her first book at the age of eleven, after which life, career and a growing family kept her busy until once again she could indulge her desire to create characters and stories—this time in romance. Having her work published is a dream come true. Visit Trish at her website: www.trishmorey.com

Recent titles by the same author:

A PRICE WORTH PAYING?
BARTERING HER INNOCENCE
THE SHEIKH'S LAST GAMBLE
DUTY AND THE BEAST

Did you know these are also available as eBooks?
Visit www.millsandboon.co.uk

With grateful thanks to Sue and Sean Delaney
from Sinclair's Gully Wines.
Thanks for your advice, your know-how,
and most of all your friendship.
Raising a glass of Rubida to you both,
Trish
xxx

CHAPTER ONE

'BE NICE TO him, Holly.'

Holly Purman smiled and put on her most innocent expression, the one she reserved for when her grandfather was asking something of her that she didn't want to give. The one that usually worked like a charm. 'When am I ever not nice to anyone?'

'I mean it,' Gus growled, refusing point-blank this time to be swayed. 'I know what you're like when you get a bee in your bonnet about something or somebody, and I reckon there's an entire hive buzzing around up there right now.'

'Nobody wears bonnets these days, Pop.' She stooped down to kiss her grandfather's creased forehead, adding with a grin, 'They're old hat.'

'This is no joking matter, Holly! I want you to take this visit from Franco Chatsfield seriously. It's a big deal, him coming all this way to talk to us, and the money he's talking—well, it could set us up for life.'

Holly sighed, abandoning the plans she had to head out to the paddock to let the sheep into the vineyard. The sheep weren't going to starve in the next thirty minutes and the winter weeds would still be waiting for them in the rows between the vines. Besides, she was hardly going to convince her grandfather that a deal with Chatsfield wasn't going to be the deal of the century without having the conversation she'd been stewing over ever since Gus had taken the phone call agreeing to some representative from Chatsfield's visiting with an offer.

She pulled up a chair opposite her grandfather and sat down, putting her hand over his where it rested on the arm of his wheelchair. 'Okay, Pop, I'll be serious. We have interest from the Chatsfield Hotel Group. This isn't so surprising, surely? After winning gold or silver at nearly every wine show going, suddenly everyone wants a piece of Purman Wines. We've had loads of interest from potential buyers from all over Australia and from that big supermarket chain in the UK, and I thought you were happy with those. So why are you so excited about some guy coming from Chatsfield? What can hooking up with them give us that none of the others can?'

'Exposure, that's what! You know as well as I do that a deal with Chatsfield will give us a global exposure we won't get through any of our other offers! Chatsfield can take our wine to the world and give it a five-star tick of approval into the deal. You can't buy that kind of promotion!'

She rubbed her temple where a pulse beat insistently beneath, wishing she'd been in the office the day the call had come in—the call her grandfather had taken in her absence and been so excited about since. She wouldn't have been so quick to agree to the visit. In fact, she would most likely have told Franco Chatsfield or whatever his name was not to waste his time and effort.

But by the time she'd found out, he was already on his way. And her grandfather was right, she'd been fuming about it ever since. She patted his hand now, willing herself to calm down before she spoke.

'Sure, Pop, you're right. We'll get international exposure if we hook up with Chatsfield, nothing surer, but is it the sort of exposure Purman Wines really wants? Every week it seems there's another scandal involving that family. What with Lucca Chatsfield caught in a...well, let's just say "compromising situation"... Do we as a quality brand want the Purman name linked with theirs? We've both worked so hard to ensure its success, and I don't want to see the Purman name dragged through the mud.'

'Chatsfield is the most prestigious hotel chain in the world!'

'It used to be, Pop. Once upon a time it used to stand for something special. It still clings to its heritage every chance it gets, but these days the brand is more synonymous with scandal than style.'

His eyes squeezed shut as he shook his head. Emphatic. 'No, no, no! That's all in the past. Things are turning around. That's what he told me. There's a new CEO in charge and the entire chain is getting a makeover. Overhauling their menu and wine list is part of the deal. They're spending big dollars, Holly, to get the very best. They're offering the big bucks. Why shouldn't we cash in on it?'

Holly gave her grandfather a wan smile. 'We've met men with fat wallets who promised the world before, Pop, remember? I don't recall you being quite so excited then.'

Gus snorted and crooked an eyebrow, his eyes still a piercing blue and sharp as a needle, although the skin around them was creased and tanned from a lifetime of working outdoors. 'Is that what this is all about? Something that happened ten years ago?' His gaze grew more intent, his expression deadly serious. 'He was never good enough for you, Holly, and you know it!'

'I know that,' she said, sucking in air at that old familiar stab of hurt, dulled now with the passage of time, but still lurking. Still hurting if she let it. And sometimes she did, just to remind herself never to be so naive again. 'But that's not what I meant. Because I recall what happened after you'd sent him packing—when he did his best to drag the Purman name through the mud. Don't you remember all those poisonous articles in the papers he wrote where he called us "Poorman Wines"? And all those calls from clients cancelling orders, worrying we couldn't deliver? Don't you remember all those phone calls from reporters believing we wouldn't be in business twelve months down the line? Do we really want to bring that kind of exposure on us again?'

'But this will be different. The money alone—'

'Money isn't the only consideration. This is about protecting our brand! If Chatsfield is trying to improve its public image, bully for them, but I don't see why we should lend our name and our success and risk losing everything we've worked to build up, just to make them look good.'

Pop shook his head, the leathery skin between his brows more creased than ever. 'It's not just about the money, I know. Just talk to him, Holly. He'll be here soon. Listen to what he has to say. Give the man a chance. Give Chatsfield a chance.'

The thought of doing a deal with them and risking what had happened before gave her the shudders. 'Why don't you talk to him if you're so keen?'

'I will. But since I'm reduced to this useless device—' he slammed the palm of one hand against the wheel '—it will be you showing him around the vineyard and the winery. It will be you explaining your vintages, that's as it should be. Because it's you everyone wants to meet— the wine whisperer. Dionysus's handmaiden, the woman who turns the humble grape into nectar of the gods.' His eyes misted over. 'My Holly.'

She sighed and squeezed his hand. 'Those wine writers talk such rubbish.'

'No, it's true. All true. You have a gift, my girl, a God-given gift for the grapes and the wine. I'm so proud of you.'

She smiled, a soft smile she hoped told him just how much she loved him, before leaning over to add a kiss to his leathery cheek for good measure. 'If it is true, it's only because you taught me everything I know.'

He caught her hand within the iron grip of his bony fingers, blinking to clear watery eyes as he turned his impassioned expression up to hers. 'Don't you see, Holly? This Chatsfield deal could be the opportunity of a lifetime.'

She could see how he'd think it so. The dollars alone were enough to make anyone's eyes water. But it could also turn out to be the biggest blunder of all time, given the parlous state of the Chatsfield family and its hotel chain.

But she didn't say so, not when her grandfather seemed so set on making a deal with them. 'I'll talk to him, Pop,' she said simply and even honestly with a smile for the man who had been the centre of her existence for so long she didn't remember a time when he hadn't been there for her. 'I'll give him a chance and I'll listen to what he has to say.'

And then I'll tell him to go to hell.

CHAPTER TWO

FRANCO CHATSFIELD DIDN'T appreciate having a gun held to his head, especially not by Christos Giatrakos—the man his father had hired in to bring his siblings into line.... *Him* into line.

He tossed away the business magazine he'd been attempting to read on the descent into Adelaide Airport, giving up all pretence of being able to focus on the words. Because the closer he got to landing, the more resentful he grew.

In normal circumstances he wouldn't have given someone like Giatrakos five minutes of his time.

In normal circumstances he would have told Giatrakos where to well and truly get off.

Except that Giatrakos's last email had stopped him in his tracks.

From: Christos.Giatrakos@TheChatsfield.com
To: Franco.Chatsfield@TheChatsfield.com
Subject: CONDITIONS OF TRUST CONTINUATION
Despite numerous attempts to make you see sense, be aware that failure to seal the deal with Purman Wines will leave me no choice but to use the power your father has given me and lock down your access to your trust funds.

This is your last warning.
C.G.

Jeopardising the income stream from the Chatsfield Family Trust was the one thing Franco couldn't let happen.

So he'd play the game by Giatrakos's rules. He'd even let Giatrakos think he'd won the day if it was that important to him. Because he'd spoken to Angus Purman and it was clear from his enthusiastic response to his offer that getting his signature was practically a done deal. No wonder, really, given he'd had one hell of a budget to play with and he'd teased Purman with that knowledge.

Getting the paperwork should be a mere formality, in which case, he'd be back in Milan with this deal sorted and signed and on that jerk CEO's desk before the ink was even dry on the contract.

And if his father—his famous father, who hadn't given him two minutes of consideration since he'd been born— had thought for a moment that he would be cowed by the prospect of sorting out a new wine contract for Chatsfield's prestige hotel chain, he had another think coming.

He might have dropped out of school at sixteen and fled the Chatsfield media circus before it could consume him, but he'd still managed to learn a thing or two along the way. Maybe his father might finally realise that?

He snorted.

Not that he cared either way.

The plane bumped through clouds on its descent and he looked out the window, searching for his first glimpse of Adelaide, but there was still no sign of anything approaching a city. Instead below him spread an undulating carpet of green dotted with tiny towns connected by winding ribbons of bitumen. There were forests of pine and the dull grey of eucalypts, interspersed with open fields, and vineyards too, marching in regimented lines across the hillsides. Somewhere down there, he figured, must be Purman's cool-climate pinot-chardonnay block that provided the fruit for their award-winning sparkling wine.

A burst of rain spattered against his window, obliterating the view, and Franco reclined back in his seat as the plane bumped its descent over the hills. Not that he had to know where exactly, because as soon as the plane landed and he cleared customs, he was heading straight to Purman's Coonawarra head office, one more short flight away. He didn't want or need to see anything else. His job was to fill in a few final details on the contract he had ready and get a signature. It wasn't like he was here to have a holiday. In fact, the sooner he'd put Giatrakos—the jerk—back in his box and ensured the funds from the Chatsfield Family Trust kept flowing where he wanted them to, the better.

Right now, that was all he cared about.

It might be winter but the weather was worse than wintry, it was foul, and Holly had come in from the vineyard to escape it while she made them both a sandwich for lunch. Above the pounding of the rain on the roof she barely registered the noise at first. Even when she did make out the distinctive whump-whump of chopper blades, she didn't pay it much attention. They weren't that far from the airfield after all, and there was a steady trade in sightseer flights, although admittedly more common in the warmer months.

But the noise grew progressively louder and closer and Holly stopped slicing cheese as a shiver of premonition zipped down her spine. Could it be him?

She grabbed a tea towel to wipe her hands as she crossed to the glass doors that looked out over acres of vines, now mostly bare and stripped of their leaves, to see a helicopter hovering above the lawns that doubled as a rudimentary helipad when occasion demanded.

Her grandfather wheeled alongside her as the chopper descended slowly to the ground.

'You reckon it's him?'

'Who else could it be? Clearly it's somebody who likes to make an entrance. It figures it'd be a Chatsfield.'

'You don't know that, Holly.'

Her hackles did.

Her bones did.

'It's him,' she said, before balling the tea towel in her hands and unceremoniously flinging it across the room to land in the sink with the same unerring certainty. She slid open the door to air that was so cold and crisp it might snap, the rain squalls moved on for now, and from the edge of the verandah they waited as the chopper's motor wound down, the blades' revolutions slowing.

And even though it was near-freezing outside, her blood simmered with resentment. Did he honestly imagine they'd be impressed at such a grand entrance?

Not likely.

The passenger door popped open and their visitor jumped out and Holly's skin prickled.

Tall, she registered. Around six foot if she wasn't mistaken, though it was hard to tell given how far he had to duck his head under the rotating blades. And then he straightened and she could see his face and he could be nothing other than a Chatsfield, with his chiselled good looks and the tendrils of his bad-boy hair flicking like serpents in the down draft from the blades.

The prickling under her skin intensified and spread until even her breasts tingled and peaked. The cold, she told herself as she clutched her arms over her chest and pressed her fingernails tight into her flesh. Damn this cold and damn this man who was smiling as if he was welcome here.

As if he imagined he was going to get a slice of Purman Wine action.

Not on her watch.

'Angus Purman?' he said, extending a hand to her grandfather. 'Franco Chatsfield. It's good to meet you.'

'Gus will do just fine,' the older man said with a nod, and Franco felt his hand enveloped by a weatherbeaten paw that housed a grip of steel. 'And this here's my granddaughter, Holly. She's the real boss of the show.'

Really? 'Holly,' he said, taking her hand in turn, and there could be no greater contrast between the two handshakes. For while the older man's had been certain, his leathery skin calloused and hard, hers was cool and way too brief to decide if that buzz he'd felt on contact had been any more than his imagination. She made no attempt to acknowledge him or return his smile, but then, she didn't look happy at all. Instead she looked— He searched for a word as he took in her khaki work pants, dusty boots and a faded long-sleeved polo jumper bearing the Purman Wines logo. *Drab.* In fact, if it wasn't for blue eyes in a make-up-free face, she'd be completely colourless.

'I apologise if my arrival has taken you unawares,' he said, realising she must be angry because she hadn't had time to get herself ready. He knew how women liked to preen.

'No, of course, we were expecting you,' the old man said genially.

'We just weren't expecting you—' the woman added, gesturing towards the helicopter '—in that.'

So she *was* angry with him. But what the hell for? 'I had to take it from Mount Gambier. Storms closed the Coonawarra airfield so my charter flight couldn't land here.'

'There were no hire cars?' Gus asked as he wheeled himself inside and gestured Franco to follow.

'No,' he said as he followed, discounting the offer he'd had of a car so tiny his knees would have been around his ears. 'At least, nothing that was suitable.'

'They were all out of Maseratis?' quipped the woman. 'I just hate it when that happens.'

'Holly!' Gus growled over his shoulder, and Franco pulled his lips into a smile in spite of his building irritation. He was here with a fistful of dollars in his pocket and a deal that anyone would be mad to turn down and yet she was acting like he wasn't welcome. What the hell was her problem?

Warmth enveloped him as he stepped into a spacious living area, a kitchen one end and a dining area dominated by a massive timber table the other, all warmed by a stone-walled fireplace pumping out the heat. Stone and timber featured largely in the interior, working in combination with the high ceilings and windows that afforded a view over the surrounding vines. And not that he'd given it much thought, but he hadn't expected to be reminded of his own stone villa in the Piacenza hills outside Milan and to actually like what he found half a world away in the southeast corner of South Australia.

'We were just about to have lunch,' Gus said. 'Why don't you sit down and join us?'

Franco held up his hands. 'I don't want to put you out,' he said, and Holly caught the gleam of a gold watch at his wrist. Ridiculously expensive gold watch, by the looks, just like the ridiculously expensive hand-stitched leather shoes on his feet. Big feet, she registered absently, and in the very next instant wished she hadn't.

Tall.

Big feet.

What did they say about tall men with big feet?

And heat that had nothing to do with the fireplace suddenly blossomed hot and heavy in her cheeks. She turned her back towards the men, launching an attack on a loaf with the bread knife, furious with herself. She didn't even like the man. Why the hell would she even think such a thing?

'A man can't be expected to do business on an empty stomach,' Gus said. 'It's no trouble, is it, Holly?'

'No trouble at all,' she said with a brightness she didn't feel. 'I do hope you're a fan of corned beef sandwiches?'

'But of course,' he said, and not for the first time, Holly wondered at his accent. She'd expected him to sound upper crust and privileged, and he did—for the most part. But every now and then there was an unexpected texture to his accent that curled the edges away from Sloane Square and headed for somewhere entirely more earthy.

Maybe because of his Italian mother? Not that it mattered. Not that she cared.

'That's the spirit,' her grandfather said. 'Holly not only makes the best wine in the district, it's a little-known fact she also makes the best sandwiches. She makes the relish herself, you know.'

'Then I am indeed fortunate. It appears I couldn't have timed my arrival better.'

A charmer, she thought as she put together a platter of doorstop sandwiches, adding this latest discovery to his list of crimes, a list that was growing longer by the minute. A Chatsfield and a charmer with a posh accent, who wore handmade shoes and gold watches and who hired helicopters when mere mortals hired cars—and usually the budget model at that.

She didn't care for charmers with fat pockets.

She didn't trust them.

She glanced over her shoulder at their guest, her father and Franco engaged in conversation. Another squall had hit, the rain coming in fat drops that belted onto the tin roof and splattered over the windows when the wind blew it horizontally under the wide verandah, and over the din, she could barely hear what they were saying. It was just a shame the noise didn't dull her vision. He'd shrugged off his jacket while her back had been turned, revealing a fine-knitted sweater that skimmed his powerful shoulders and chest like a second skin. Some tall people looked like weeds. Not Franco. He looked hard packed. Built. He seemed to own the space around him. Not an easy thing in this room when he was surrounded by so much of it.

All the more reason to resent him, she told herself as she set the plate of sandwiches on the table and retreated to the safety of the kitchen to snap on the kettle, watching him take a sandwich in his hands.

Long-fingered hands.

Long-fingered hands with big thumbs.

He'd taken her hand in his and she could still feel the tingle under her skin, the zap that had reminded her of science class where they'd scuffed shoes on the carpet and reached out a hand. It had been fun then.

It wasn't fun now.

She lifted her eyes and caught him watching her and sensation skittered down her spine. She spun, looking out the window, looking anywhere but at him, wondering what was wrong with her.

'You're not eating,' he said.

She shook her head, wondering what had happened to her appetite. She'd felt hungry when she'd first come in from outside, but she was too wound up now to eat, too busy thinking he should never have come. Wishing she'd taken the call and told him not to. Thinking there was no point to all of this…

'You must take Franco out to the vineyard,' Gus said, 'when this latest shower has passed. You should show him our terra rossa soil, and why our grapes do so well.'

'Pop, have you looked out the window? I'm not sure it's a good day to take anyone outside.' Especially if it meant being alone with him.

'Nonsense!' He looked at their guest. 'Franco would never have come all this way without wanting to see everything there is to know about the vineyard and the winery.'

'Of course,' he conceded, his words and smile both tighter than a trellis wire. 'Naturally, I would appreciate seeing as much as I can while I am here.'

'Excellent,' said Gus, slapping the palms of his hands on his legs, triumphant. Holly wasn't so convinced. Their guest hadn't exactly jumped at the chance. Maybe he was afraid of getting his pretty shoes wet. 'Now, you'd better get going before the next squall hits. Holly will find you a coat.'

Franco rose to his feet.

'Oh, and, Gus, after the tour, perhaps we could sit down together and go over the details of Chatsfield Hotel's offer?'

Holly's head snapped around. So here it was. 'You sure don't waste any time, do you, Mr Chatsfield?'

'Please call me Franco. And no, I don't like wasting time, neither yours nor mine. In fact, I have a contract with me all ready to be signed. I told your grandfather on the phone the terms were generous and I can guarantee we'll better any other offer on the table. I'd appreciate the opportunity to discuss the proposal with you in more detail.'

'I look forward to it,' said a bright-eyed Gus, who was

looking like a kid itching to unwrap the biggest present under the Christmas tree. 'I'm sorry I can't come out myself while I'm confined to this infernal thing. Holly, I'll be in the study doing some paperwork. Let me know when you get back and we'll all sit down together and see if we can't do business.'

The sky outside offered a rare patch of blue and Holly reckoned they had ten minutes before the next bank of dark cloud rumbled overhead and dropped its load.

'This is going to ruin your snazzy shoes,' Holly warned as she climbed into her creaky-with-age Driza-Bone oilskin. No way would his feet fit into Gus's boots.

'It's no problem, really,' he said. 'They're only shoes.'

She smiled at that as she pulled on her knee-high gumboots.

Only someone used to buying hand-crafted shoes would think they were only shoes. Clearly the Chatsfields had more money than sense.

Another crime added to the list.

She strode before him across the sodden lawn in her work boots, hands wedged deeply in the pockets of her coat. She didn't need to look over her shoulder to know Franco was right behind her. She could feel him in the prickling heat of her skin. She could sense him in the swirling air of her wake—thick, smug air—just one more dark cloud on a stormy day. At least this cloud would soon blow away. Back to his privileged world and his scandal-ridden existence.

'Be nice to him,' Pop had told her, and she reined in on the resentment that bubbled up under her skin at him being here, at his film-star good looks and his entitled accent and his damned big feet and thumbs, but nowhere near enough to quell it completely. No. She could not find it in herself to be nice. But she supposed she could at least try for civil. He wasn't going to be here long. She could do civil.

At least until he put his offer on the table.

'We have around fifty hectares of prime Coonawarra land under vines,' she started, and Franco tuned out, toying with a new and unexpected discovery. Because he'd seen her smile back in the mud room, maybe only because she'd been laughing at his shoes, but still she'd smiled. And it had been a revelation, because she was almost pretty when she smiled, when she let her frosty guard down and let the light play about her blue eyes and tweak her lips. They'd become startling blue eyes when she smiled, a burst of colour when she was otherwise clad in so much drabness. Who would have thought it?

She led him towards an old stone building nestled into a stand of enormous gum trees that served as their cellar door, smoke rising from its chimney, and all the while Holly talked and Franco only half listened, letting the details of the varieties and acreage and yields wash over him, details he didn't need to know because soon he'd be gone and would never need to give Purman Wines or its cantankerous Miss Drab another thought.

Until then, he guessed, he would just have to endure it.

They stopped at a cutting in the soil, where the ground had been scooped away in a wedge shape to reveal the rich red soil lying atop its white limestone base, and she began to explain terra rossa soil, and Franco's patience snapped.

'Save me the lecture. I know what terra rossa means.' *Dio*, if it wasn't enough that his mother was Italian, he'd lived in Italy for the past decade.

'Oh, I'm sorry. I assumed you'd grown up in England.'

'I did,' he said tersely, glancing over the massive shed beyond that housed the winery proper, suspecting that she was headed there next and already impatient for it to be over. He'd only agreed to come along because he'd worried they might have thought it looked odd if he hadn't shown an interest.

But now he looked back across the vineyards, in the direction of the homestead, thinking he'd played Mr Cooperative long enough. It was time to get down to business if he wanted this thing wrapped up today.

'Thank you for the tour, Ms Purman. I think we should be heading back now.'

Holly blinked those blue eyes. 'The tour isn't actually finished yet.'

'Gus is waiting for us.'

'He knows we'll be a while.'

'I'd rather not keep him waiting.'

She drew in a short sharp breath, laced with frustration.

'But you haven't even tasted the wines or seen the winery yet.'

'The wine is good. Otherwise I wouldn't be here with a contract in my pocket. Don't you understand? Chatsfield Hotels wants to buy your entire vintage, down to every lock, stock and French oak barrel. We're not about to change our minds whatever you show me. We'd be better off using our time getting agreement over the contract.'

Her blue eyes flashed like sun on ice, as cold and sharp as the wind that needled around his ears. She swept one arm around in an arc over the vineyard. 'I knew you weren't interested in a tour. But then, you're not actually interested in any of this, are you?' She was staring right at him, right into him, shaking her head while those ice-blue eyes continued to try to slice him to pieces with laser precision.

'Don't take it personally. I'm here to do business, not play tourist.'

'Have you ever tasted our wines?'

'Is that relevant?'

'You're unbelievable! I bet you don't even know the first thing about wine!'

The hackles on the back of his neck rose. If she only knew. But he wasn't about to tell her. 'I know a bit about wine, yes.'

She smiled then, if you could call it a smile, because there was no light dancing in those blue eyes. They were cold and glassy and filled with bad intentions. 'You know "a bit" about wine then?' she repeated, nodding. 'An expert indeed. So I guess you know there are two kinds of wine, right? Red and white?'

He felt the skin pull taut over the bones of his cheeks, felt his lips draw back into a snarl, but his voice, when it came, was tight and purposeful and betrayed nothing of how close he was to losing his control. 'I wouldn't quite put it that way.'

'Oh, of course not,' she said, any pretence at civility abandoned and left smoking in the heat of her delivery. 'I was forgetting. Because there are actually three kinds of wine. You are a Chatsfield after all. You weren't just born with a silver spoon in your mouth, you were born clutching a champagne flute in your hand.'

His hands formed fists, and if there'd been a champagne flute in either of them, it would have shattered, like his control, into tiny pieces.

Nobody judged him.

Not since his father had made it clear he didn't need a son and Franco had subsequently dropped out of Eton and stormed off to Italy in rebellion had he been judged and found guilty by anyone other than himself.

And he was his own harshest critic.

So he was hardly likely to sit back and be found guilty by the likes of this woman.

She knew nothing of him.

Nothing!

The scar in his side ached as a familiar guilt assailed him—guilt for when he'd discovered what he'd unwittingly left behind in England—guilt for the years he'd lost and the pain he'd caused. Guilt that he'd been unable to save his child's life just twelve short months later.

Nikki.

And pain lanced him as sharp and deep as it had that day, ten years before, when he'd learned that everything he'd done—everything he'd given—had come to nothing.

Curse the woman!

She knew nothing. But nothing in his agreement with Christos Giatrakos said he had to educate her, to explain. Nothing in his agreement said he had to apologise. He didn't want her understanding or her forgiveness. All he needed was her damned signature on the dotted line.

'Chatsfield Hotels want to buy your wines and we're prepared to pay top dollar for the privilege.' His voice was as calm and reasonable as he could manage under the circumstances, a thin veneer of civility over a mountain of reason and he'd make her appreciate just how much reason if it killed him. 'We'll not only purchase the entire vintage, but your precious wines will be showcased exclusively in the executive lounges of our hotels all over the world. You will never get a better deal. So why the hell won't you even attempt to listen to what I have to say?'

Her chin kicked up. 'Maybe because I'm not interested in what you have to say. If Chatsfield Hotels were actually serious about buying Purman Wines, they should have sent someone who knows something about wine and winemaking—not some messenger boy!'

If she'd slapped his cold cheek with the palm of her hand it couldn't have stung as much as her ice-cold words, and far from the first time he cursed Christos Giatrakos for putting him in this position.

If he didn't need to seal this deal—didn't need this woman's cooperation—Franco could have climbed back in the helicopter and left then and there.

But he couldn't leave. He wouldn't give frosty Ms Purman and her ice-blue eyes the satisfaction. She might be standing in his way now, frustrating his efforts to get a quick closure, but he'd get what he'd come for.

He had to. He could not risk losing his distribution from the Chatsfield Family Trust. He would do a deal with the devil himself to save it.

So he swallowed down cold air smelling of damp earth and wet grass. He could not afford to antagonise this woman any more than he clearly already had, so he would not rise to her bait, but that didn't mean he must take her barbs and insults lying down. He might at least call her on it.

'Do you treat all your potential customers like this, Ms Purman? Or are you singling me out for special treatment?'

The woman smiled, and now it was more than light that danced in her ice-blue, scathing eyes, there was cold, hard satisfaction. She was enjoying this. 'I'm afraid I *am* singling you out. Does that make you feel special, Mr Chatsfield?'

Her brazen admission sent white-hot fury pumping through his veins and pounding at his temples, hammering at his skull like he wished he could hammer sense into her. He was here to bestow the biggest contract this woman was ever likely to see in her lifetime, and yet she couldn't have been less welcoming were he the grim reaper come to harvest her grandfather's soul.

Somehow he managed to force a smile to his features, although he had to work hard to move his lips beyond a tight thin line.

'I think we're wasting our time here. I think we should go and talk to your grandfather. At least he seems a little less averse to doing business with the Chatsfield Hotel Group.'

'Fine, we'll do what you want. We'll go and see Pop.' She smiled again and, unlike him, seemed to have no problem finding the necessary muscles to make it stick. 'But you see, we're a partnership, Pop and me, and you need both our signatures on that contract. So I warn you now, don't go getting your hopes up.'

CHAPTER THREE

'THIS IS RIDICULOUS!'

Franco Chatsfield was not a happy man.

They'd been talking all afternoon it seemed, Franco talking the deal up, dollar signs plastered thickly to every word, while Gus had listened eagerly, hanging on every gold-plated promise. Holly, meanwhile, had been busy hosing down Franco's excess enthusiasm and finding flaws in the deal and still Franco's signature was the only one so far on the contract.

It hadn't been easy. Franco Chatsfield had made his offer sound better than good. He'd made it sound like it was the deal of a lifetime as he'd laid out figures and facts and promised an endless stream of dollars if only they would both sign on the dotted line.

To Gus it must have sounded like a dream come true, the culmination and validation of his life's work.

Holly could understand why. She could see that in isolation, if the money was all that mattered, then the dollars looked amazing.

But that didn't mean she was about to buckle. There was more to success than dollars, and she remembered a time when adverse publicity had almost ruined them. As long as the offer was coming from Chatsfield, a once-grand name now more synonymous with headlines and scandal, it was hard to see how they could ever do business.

Why didn't her grandfather see it that way?

Half an hour ago the helicopter had departed, and Franco, stony-faced, had watched it take off and still the discussions wore on, and all the time she'd watched the skin of his face pull progressively tighter across his bones, until the tendons in his neck had become taut and corded and stained red with tension and he'd looked like a volcano about to erupt.

And then Gus had excused himself, promising to be back, and before Holly could wonder what he'd gone off in search of, Franco had erupted. He'd slammed his fist on the table and leapt from his chair, his eyes wild and jaw rigid as finally he gave in to the temptation to blow. 'A complete and utter waste of time,' he snarled as he prowled before the fire like a lion cheated of its kill. 'We're getting nowhere,' he said, his back to her as he raked fingers through his long hair. He spun around and pinned his cold, winter-grey eyes on her, and she was struck anew by his height and power and his ability to eat up the space around him and shrink it down till there was just him and the fire and a hot lick of flame she could almost feel on her skin. 'What is your problem?' he growled. It wasn't a question. It was an accusation.

Vaguely she was aware of a phone ringing but then it stopped and she knew Gus must have picked it up in the study.

Franco was still staring at her, hostile eyes demanding an answer. Holly didn't bother with a smile. While there was a certain satisfaction in knowing that she'd stymied this man's smug expectations of walking out of here with exactly what he wanted, something told her that smiling would not go down well right now.

But that didn't mean she had to cower.

'Seems to me, I'm not the one with a problem.'

'You think? Because you would have to be the most intransigent, uncooperative, stubborn woman I have ever met.'

'Why, thank you.'

'That wasn't a compliment.'

She arched an eyebrow over one glacier-blue eye. 'I take them where I can find them.'

He snorted and turned away. Little wonder. The way she looked in those oversize, drab work clothes, compliments were no doubt thin on the ground.

He strode past the fireplace. He needed this contract signed and he'd get it signed, come hell or high water, and he refused to be beaten by a woman who'd dug her heels in from the very start. But how to make her shift her position?

The old man was already in his pocket. He just had to sway her.

The old man...

And he spun back around, finding a new weapon in his arsenal, a new direction from which to attack now that the old man had left the room and they were alone. 'Why are you so against this deal?' he demanded. 'Your grandfather is keen to do business. So why are *you* so adamantly opposed to doing a deal with Chatsfield?'

She crossed her arms over her chest, her body language confirming just how far closed was her mind, although the act of defiance also revealed something else—something as unexpected as the transformation in her features when she smiled. For there was shape under that shapeless Purman sweater. Curves. And the heat of his anger morphed into a different kind of heat as his body stirred in response. He willed the reaction away, as unlikely as it was unwanted, as she said, 'We can do better.'

'Financially?' he challenged, his eyes back on hers, his focus back on track. 'Not a chance.'

'It may surprise you to learn that there's more to life than money, Mr Chatsfield. We're building up a prize-winning brand here at Purmans—a prestige brand. I don't want to see that put at risk.'

'So you'd turn down the best offer you're ever likely to get, because you're afraid?'

She was on her feet in an instant, her jaw rigid, her blue eyes defiant. 'You say afraid. I say once bitten, twice shy. Do you think you're the only one to see the value of our wines? Ten years ago someone else with big pockets tried to buy us out—he promised riches beyond our imagination too.' He'd offered more besides that still made her ill to think about. 'But when Gus finally turned him down, he did everything he could to ruin us. "Poorman's Wines," he labelled us, every chance he got, undermining all we'd built up, threatening relations with our best stockists and our most loyal clients alike.

'It's taken ten long years of rebuilding, Mr Chatsfield, and you blithely walk in here and expect us to get tangled up with a business that is more likely to feature in the gossip columns of the scandal sheets than the business pages? I don't think so!'

She was flushed, her fists clenched tight at her sides and her eyes like braziers burning with cold blue flame and it was like he was seeing her for the first time.

She was magnificent.

And part of him wanted to goad her, to prod and needle her some more and see more of that passion that transformed this drab little mouse of a woman into a tigress that might have been fighting to protect her cubs.

Part of him wondered where else she might turn into a

tigress and what it might be like to have that passion unleashed on him.

While the sane, logical part of him wondered if he'd gone mad. She was so very not his type of woman.

And he had a contract to get signed.

'Don't you think it strange that your grandfather doesn't appear to share your concerns?'

She shook her head. 'Gus is looking at the offer through a Vaseline lens. His view is distorted and blurred around the edges. He has this romantic notion of Chatsfield Hotels that was shaped some time last century when the chain had a reputation worth having. And as much as I respect my grandfather's opinion, this time it's proving not to be based on good business sense.'

'The Chatsfield Hotel Group is hardly a "chain." You make it sound like some two-star budget deal.'

'Do I? Well, whatever you call it, unfortunately Pop's missed just how far its reputation has slipped over the past few decades. He's not quite up to speed on the latest trashy magazine gossip.'

'Whereas you, on the other hand, are?'

Her eyes sparkled with ice-cold crystals. 'I go to the dentist twice a year. Seems there isn't an edition of the magazines published where one or more of the Chatsfield clan doesn't feature front and centre.'

He shook his head, cursing the fact he belonged to a family that had, for as long as he could remember, insisted on playing out its sordid lives on the front page of every scandal sheet going. If his family was the issue, how the hell would he ever convince her to sign?

'You treated this deal with contempt from the start. And by not being the slightest bit prepared to take heed of what your grandfather wants, you treat your grandfather and his wishes with contempt.'

'Pop will get over the disappointment the moment he sees the next Chatsfield scandal unfold in all its gory, glossy details—I'll make sure he does—and then he'll be glad he never put pen to paper on this deal. Besides, it's not like we have to sign. There are other offers on the table.'

'Like ours? Like hell.'

'No, they're not like yours. They're solid deals with reputable parties, parties we'll be happy to pin the Purman name to. And even if the money doesn't quite attain the same dizzy heights, at least we can be sure our name won't end up in the gutter—unlike some of your famous siblings.'

A gust of wind rattled the windows and the fire crackled and spat fiery sparks that nowhere near rivalled the heated embers that flew at her from Franco's cold grey eyes, and Holly marvelled at the contradiction of fire and ice as he glared across the room at her, the twitch of a muscle in his jaw his only movement.

Intransigent, he'd called her.

Maybe Franco was right.

But she had a damned good reason. And maybe she didn't understand completely why Gus didn't see it the same way, when he'd been there ten years ago and he knew how hard it had been to rebuild their name after they'd been so publicly trashed, but that didn't mean she had to lower her standards.

'I'm sorry, Franco,' she said, suddenly tired of the fighting, and the tension this man added to the room by his mere presence and just wanting him gone, 'but there's no point discussing this any longer. I'm not going to change my mind. You're simply not the kind of person I want to do business with. End of story.'

It might have been too, if Gus hadn't wheeled himself back into the room a moment later, oblivious to the tension between the two warring parties, an old cardboard box perched on his lap. 'That was Tom on the phone.'

He was frowning, Holly noticed, the worry lines on his face noticeably deeper, and for a moment she forgot about Franco. 'What's wrong?'

'Tom can't make it.'

'What? But he promised he'd be here tomorrow.' A team of workers had been engaged to start in a couple of weeks when the younger vines would need work, but Tom was an expert who'd agreed to help her with their most precious low-yielding vines that she wouldn't trust to anyone but family.

Gus shook his head. 'Susie's ill. Breast cancer. She starts chemo in Adelaide Monday. He's sorry, but...' He shook his head.

'Oh, Pop.' She crossed the room and knelt down beside him and enclosed one of his hands in hers. Gus had lost Esme to cancer twenty years ago when Holly was just a kid in primary school and Tom and Susie had been there, supporting him, at her funeral.

Losing Esme had almost killed him. He'd once told her that if he hadn't had Holly to look after, it probably would have. And now, for it to happen to a friend... 'That's horrible news.'

'I told him things have improved. That Susie's chances were better now than they would have been twenty years ago.'

She blinked away tears. She wanted to hug her grandfather and squeeze him tight and she would have, if they didn't have this wretched visitor, and so she simply said, 'That'll help, Pop. I know it will help.'

He nodded on a long sigh, rubbing his bristly jaw with one hand. 'Yeah, but it's gonna mess with our plans too,

Holly. Where are we going to find someone else to help you prune at such short notice?'

'Let's talk about it later,' she said, wanting to close down the conversation as she stole a glance at Franco, wishing that this stranger didn't have to bear witness to everything that was going on in their lives right now. 'Tom's not the only one around here who can prune.' Even though he would be nigh on impossible to replace at this time of year. 'What's in the box?'

'Oh,' he said, as if he'd forgotten it was sitting there in his lap. 'I found it. Devil's own thing to find. Come and see. Franco, I think you'll find this interesting too.'

Holly followed her grandfather warily to the table, curiosity warring with frustration. She didn't expect whatever was in that box to make any difference to anything, but she was curious what he'd found.

Gus peeled back the flaps of the box. 'Photographs?' What on earth was Gus thinking? For the box was full to the brim of old photos, sepia mixed in with black-and-white and some, more recent, in colour. He started spreading them out on the table, family photos going back decades and pictures taken at harvest or in the winery. Gus worked furiously, clearly searching for something.

But why did he think Franco might find it interesting?

'It took me forever to find them,' Gus continued. 'I figured they were somewhere in the storeroom but I had no idea where. Your grandmother always planned to organise them into albums, but there was always something else to do. There never seemed to be enough time. Oh, look,' he said, passing her one. 'Here you are at the beach. You must have been all of three years old in that one.'

She blinked down at the photo in her hands. The photographic paper was thick and curled on the corners with age but there she was, sitting on her mother's lap in the sand, the Holly of three chubby in her floral one-piece, grinning up at the camera with a spade in one hand, bucket in the other.

Her eye was drawn instinctively to the woman who was her mother.

Holly looked at her smiling face, touched a fingertip to a face she wished she could remember other than from seeing it in photographs.

'Ah,' announced Gus, delighted. 'Here it is!' Followed almost immediately by his handing it to her with a growl. 'No, that's not the one I'm looking for,' and more fervent digging.

Holly took it anyway. It was a smaller version of one she knew well, a photo of her parents holding her as a newborn, one they'd had blown up and had sat framed on the mantelpiece until Holly at ten had decided it belonged on the dressing table in her bedroom and spirited it away one day.

If Gus had noticed, he'd never remarked on the move.

She looked at them now, the happy couple smiling at the camera, the baby in a long christening gown fringed with lace.

And she could even see the resemblance in her Dad's smile to Pop's. Oh, yeah, she thought as she studied the photo, that was definitely Pop's smile her father was wearing. And those were her eyes her mother sported. Turquoise-blue eyes under blonde hair.

And not for the first time she wished she could remember more than what faded photographs could tell her, remember her mother's scent as she hugged her tight, or the tickling rasp of her father's cheek when he'd kissed her goodnight.

They'd been ripped from her when she was far too young to form any real memories. A tear squeezed from

her eye and she fought it back as she remembered their
visitor. Now was hardly the time to be sniffling over old
photographs.

'Why did you bring them out now, Pop? What are you
looking for?'

'And why did you think I might be interested?'

He was standing behind her, Holly realised with a start,
her skin prickling all over. Sometime while she'd been absorbed in the old photos, he'd left the fireplace and now he
was standing right behind her. So close that she dare not
turn her head. So close that it seemed like he'd brought the
heat of the fire along with him until it infused her cheeks
and seared the air in her lungs.

Did he have to stand so damned close?

It wasn't like it was anything to do with him.

'Because somewhere in here,' Gus said, 'I know
there's... Ah!' His gaze focused as he pulled something
from the pile and passed it to Holly. 'I knew it! I just knew
it. You see?'

Holly didn't see. Not at first. It was a cutting from a
newspaper, stained browned with the passage of years,
with her mother and father standing outside a building,
the bride's hand to her head as her veil was lifted horizontally by the breeze, the photograph perfectly capturing the
moment as the groom reached a hand out for the wayward
veil too, laughing along with her, and so focused on each
other that it took Holly for ever to shift her eyes and see
the awning over their heads—and to recognise the name
on that awning.

No!

She blinked but there was no denying it.

'I...I don't understand,' she said, looking up at her
grandfather.

'It's true,' he said. 'Your mother and father were married at the Chatsfield Hotel in Sydney, on their opening weekend.'

'But how? Why?' It was news to Holly. Unbelievable news. As far as she'd known, the vineyard and winery had provided no more than a modest income until recently, when their wines had really begun to find success and acclaim. It seemed unlikely that they could ever have afforded to get married in a Chatsfield Hotel and one all the way over in Sydney. 'It must have cost a fortune.'

'It cost them nothing. One of those big women's magazines ran a nationwide contest to celebrate the opening. They asked people to write in saying why they deserved to hold their wedding celebration there.

'Your mother entered. She never thought she'd win, but there you go.'

'May I?' asked Franco, leaning over her, his long-fingered hand reaching for the photograph, and she caught his scent, of damp leather and red soil and fire-warmed masculine skin. She let him take the cutting, if only because she'd expected it meant he'd move back then, out of her sphere, away from her too-acute senses and heated blood. And when he failed to move anywhere near enough away, she took matters into her own hands, sliding from her chair, finding sanctuary in the straight lines and practical functionality of the kitchen. The bench at her back felt reassuringly solid and real in a world rapidly going off kilter, the air untainted by the evocative scent of a man she couldn't afford to like.

'And Mum won it.' She wasn't just dispirited. She was blindsided.

'She did indeed. She won the wedding, the reception— they flew us all over and back for the wedding and put us up. And Tanya and Richard got to enjoy the weekend in the honeymoon suite. All on the house.'

He looked down at the cutting with a shake of his head. 'I wish we had more of the wedding photos, but something happened to the film and they were ruined. Your mother was so disappointed.'

'And so it seems,' Franco said with a smile that said he knew the scales had just come down in his favour, 'that we have something in common. There is history between our respective families. Marketing will love it.'

'Why didn't you tell me, Pop?' she said, ignoring their suddenly smug visitor. She didn't want to hear they had something in common. She didn't want to think about their shared history or to have him witness hers—to see her as a three-year-old at the beach. To see her parents' wedding photos, regardless of where they were married.

She didn't want him here, period. 'Why did you wait until now to tell me?'

Her grandfather shrugged, sagging into his wheelchair and suddenly looking ten years older. 'It never came up, lovey, not when you were small. It was a detail that didn't seem important back then, not when we had more important things on our minds. And I guess, in time, it was a detail that just got missed.'

'But you must have remembered, after Franco called. You must have realised. But you said nothing.'

Moisture sheened her grandfather's eyes and she could feel an answering dampness welling up in her own. 'I wanted you to make up your own mind. This is your business as much as it is mine, Holly. In fact, you're the future of Purman Wines and I should probably butt out.'

'No!'

He put a hand up to stop her. 'Just hear me out. I should probably butt out, but I can't. I think this deal is a good one for not only the money but for the prestige it could bring, and I know we disagree on that. But before you make your final decision, I wanted you to know why I am so in favour of this deal. Your mum and dad were married in the Chatsfield Sydney, Holly. It was a perfect day, and they were so, so happy. And they'd be so proud knowing Chatsfield had singled Purman Wines out for this honour. They'd be so proud of you and what you've achieved.'

Unfair.

'Oh, Pop.' She bit her lips tight between her teeth, trying to hold herself together. No wonder he'd been so keen all along. No wonder he'd seen the Chatsfield name as some kind of Holy Grail when her parents' wedding there must have seemed like a fairytale. But he was holding on to some kind of vision of Chatsfield's as it was, back in the glory days.

'I'm sorry, Holly. Maybe I was wrong. Maybe I shouldn't have said anything at all.'

She dragged in a breath before she could speak as she shook her head. 'No. It's okay.' But it wasn't okay. Because while her reasons for denying Chatsfield a deal with Purman Wines hadn't changed, what she knew it meant to Gus had.

It wasn't just the deal of a lifetime to him. It was a link to a time when his son—and her father—was alive. It was a name he associated with one of the happiest times in his life.

Was it any wonder he wanted to go with the deal?

But where did that leave her?

Across the table, Franco saw his opportunity. It had been there, hovering in the back of his mind ever since the old man had returned, but it had been only a shadow of an idea then, a mere wisp of 'what if?' But now that shadow of an idea had grown and found form and substance and, best of all, weight.

The old man was already in his pocket courtesy of an emotional attachment to the hotels. Here was a gold-plated opportunity to screw the granddaughter down and lock this contract well and truly up.

It would take time, of course, more time than he'd initially allowed. But it would be time well spent if it guaranteed the funding to Nikki's Ward.

'I thank you for sharing that, Gus, and I appreciate the fact you've given me a good hearing today. But your granddaughter has good reason for being wary of this deal.' Gus looked up, surprised. Holly looked suspicious. 'She wants what's best for Purman Wines, I understand that. I respect her for it.'

'What are you saying?' Gus said, looking crestfallen. 'You're not withdrawing your offer?'

He smiled. 'No. I'm offering you a better one.'

'It's not just about the money,' Holly said. 'I told you that.'

He nodded. 'You did. You also told me that I wasn't the kind of person you wanted to do business with.' He paused, letting that sink in. 'Let me prove to you that I am.'

Gus seemed intrigued as he looked from their visitor to his granddaughter, a frown tugging his shaggy brows together. He'd missed that part of the conversation. 'And how do you intend to do that?'

'You're down a worker. You need someone to help you prune. I'm volunteering for the job.'

CHAPTER FOUR

THE BREATH HOLLY had been holding burst free on a laugh. To think she'd almost been worried for a moment! 'That's good,' she said, pausing for air. 'That's funny!'

Gus wheeled himself closer. 'Hear him out, Holly. Listen to what the man has to say.' And to Franco, 'Now, what exactly are you proposing?'

'Oh, come on, Pop. The man knows nothing about vineyards. I doubt he's ever had to work a day in his life. Sorry, Chatsfield, I'm afraid I'm not looking for a work experience student.'

'I can prune.'

'You can?'

'Pop, no. Seriously?'

He hushed her by holding up one hand. 'Now, Franco, pruning vines like ours is a specialised job. We don't trust our low-yield high-quality grapes to machines. It's all hand pruning here. Where have you pruned?' Gus's voice cut over the top.

Holly crossed her arms and glared at Franco. This was ridiculous. They were wasting time. She should be on the phone chasing up someone to replace Tom, not listening to the wild imaginings of a spoiled rich kid who probably didn't know a hard day's work if it slapped him in the face.

'A vineyard in the Piacenza region of Italy, not far from Milan.'

'You've worked there?'

He smiled. 'You could say that. I own it.'

Silence descended so suddenly his words might have been a thunderclap.

Gus recovered first. 'You own a vineyard in Italy?'

'I do. We grow some local varietals. Malvasia, Barbera, along with some merlot and pinot noir.'

'And you didn't think to mention this before?'

'I didn't think it relevant. This deal is between Chatsfield Hotels and Purman Wines, nothing to do with my business interests.'

Holly was beyond angry. 'You couldn't even mention it in polite conversation?' He'd let her think he knew nothing of vines or wine. He'd let her accuse him of the same and not corrected her. He'd cut short the tour like it was an imposition on his precious time and not something he was interested in in the least. What was she supposed to think?

'I'm sorry. I didn't realise we'd had a polite conversation.'

Bastard.

'You could have said something!'

'I was here to broker a deal and I was under the impression Chatsfield's offer would be welcome. I didn't realise small talk was expected.'

'You made no effort!'

'You think if I had, Ms Purman, it might have made you more amenable to my offer? I think not.'

Gus grunted. 'True enough, Holly.' His eyes narrowed then, homing in on Franco. 'But can you really prune?'

'I'll be honest with you, Gus, the past couple of years I've spent more time in the boardroom than in amongst the vines, but yes, I can prune and I used to be a star pruner.

All our estate vines are hand pruned. I spent more than
ten years hand pruning every season.'

Holly felt the ground beneath her shifting so fast she
was battling to keep up. 'Oh, Pop, this is mad! You can't
seriously be thinking of agreeing to this.'

'No? And why not, Holly? We're short an experienced
worker. You know yourself how long it takes to train someone and get them up to speed. Years.'

'But he's…a Chatsfield! And whatever flimsy connection he has to this supposed vineyard in Italy—'

'The estate exists, Ms Purman. And I assure you, it's
mine.'

'Then why are you offering to do this, if you've got your
own vineyard back in Italy? How can you afford to offer
us your services and your time? Why would you do that?
What's in it for you?'

'There's something in it for me, of course. I need this
deal finalised. So I'll replace Tom and help you prune. And
when the pruning's done and dusted, to your satisfaction,
of course, then you will sign the contract.'

'But—'

'No. You're the one who made it clear you'd never do
business with a Chatsfield and that anyone with the Chatsfield name should be tarred with the same brush. I'd like
the opportunity to show you that you can't just write us all
off that way. I'd like the opportunity to prove that you can
do business with a Chatsfield and not regret it.'

'That's not the only reason I'm not in favour of this deal
and you know it.'

'True, you're also worried about the scandals that my
siblings have brought upon themselves from time to time,
and their impact on the Chatsfield name. You're worried
the Purman name might be dragged down in the fallout.
But I can tell you that you have nothing to fear. You will

no doubt choose not to believe me. But in the time it takes to prune—how many weeks will that be? Two? Four?'

'Six,' she snapped. 'At least.'

That long? A moment's hesitation before he nodded. 'Even better. Six weeks will be perfect. And if there are any scandals involving my family—any at all in that time—then you can choose to walk away from the deal, regardless of how far along we are with the pruning. Otherwise, at the end of six weeks, you sign the contract, and the deal between Chatsfield and Purman Wines is done. Do we have a deal?'

'I like it!' said Gus with a chortle as he slapped the flat of his hand against one leg. 'It solves everything. What do you say, Holly?'

Holly couldn't say anything. Not right now. She was too busy working out how she'd lost an advantage that had seemed to her, such a very short time ago, as unassailable.

She'd had the high moral ground. But the rock-solid ground she'd been so sure of minutes ago had turned to quicksand.

They were both waiting, Gus and Franco, watching her, waiting for her response. And damn them both, she wasn't about to go down without a fight. 'Surely you have family back home who will be expecting you?'

Something dark scudded across his cool grey eyes, gone as quickly as it appeared. 'No.'

'Business interests that need looking after?'

'They'll manage.'

'What if you're rubbish at pruning?'

'Then the deal is off. But I assure you, I'm not.'

'You'll have to stay for the entire time.'

'Of course.'

'However long it takes.'

'I realise that.'

'And not just being here. Contributing. We don't accept passengers.'

His smile grew wider. 'I wouldn't expect you to.'

And all of a sudden she'd run out of ifs and buts and terms and conditions.

She swallowed hard.

Hard down on her disappointment.

Hard down on her pride.

'Then I suppose we could give you a trial.'

And Gus clapped his hands together as he belted out a laugh. 'Well, it's all settled then, looks like we've got ourselves a deal!'

Was it settled? Nothing in Holly's mind felt settled. Instead it was scattered, a mess of question marks when there should be full stops.

She'd been moments away from being rid of this man of the cool grey eyes and the too-big feet, moments from freedom, and suddenly events had overtaken her and the goal posts had shifted.

Because Franco was staying and certainty had departed.

It was supposed to be the other way around.

It was Gus who insisted on cracking open a bottle of Rubida, their best sparkling wine, and proposing a toast to celebrate the deal. It was no consolation that Franco finally got to taste their wine whether he wanted to or not. It was no consolation that he thought the wine was good.

No consolation at all.

She would have liked it better if he'd screwed up his face and turned tail and run thinking that someone at head office had made a horrendous mistake. Although she knew for a fact that her wines were amongst the best out there and that there was no mistake.

And it was also Gus who decided Franco should stay

in the cottage they had prepared for Tom's arrival. Maybe it was a logical decision, but it meant he'd be living here on the property as well as working here for six weeks. Six long weeks of potentially seeing him every day. Six long weeks of feeling that itching prickle and that annoying heat under her skin. Then again, it could have been worse, Holly mused as she collected up a basket of breakfast supplies from the pantry—Gus could have invited him to stay at the house.

Perish the thought.

By the time Holly picked up her car keys to drop Franco at the cottage, the clouds had blown away and the wintry day had turned into frosty night. She welcomed the bite of the chill air against her overheated skin as she led Franco to the four-wheel drive, shoes crunching on the gravel, while she wished the cold air could similarly work some kind of magic on improving her mood. Six weeks of working alongside this man.

It didn't bear thinking about.

She stashed the basket on the back seat of the four-wheel drive before climbing into the driver's seat. The heavy door slammed shut behind her.

Damned right.

Exactly how her life felt right now. Slammed shut. All options closed.

'Ms Purman? Are you all right?'

Clearly not. Holly blinked. She'd been sitting, staring at the steering wheel and hadn't even noticed Franco climb in. 'I'm fine,' she lied through a jaw so rigid by now it was hard to talk.

He clicked in his seatbelt and his elbow brushed against hers and she flinched, feeling a jolt to her senses.

Just peachy, she thought, pulling her arms in tight against her body as she turned the key in the ignition, hating how all of a sudden she was confined in a car with a man who seemed as big as a mountain. And she hated how the air around her didn't smell of wet oilskins or muddy feet but seemed flavoured with his scent instead, of warm man and wood smoke and there was some kind of cologne mixed in there as well, something spicy and masculine and no doubt expensive. She rammed the car into First and let go the accelerator too quickly and the vehicle lurched and hopped. His fault, she thought, distracting her with that scent.

She wound down her window a couple of inches. The air was so cold it almost hurt to breathe, but it also didn't smell like him.

No contest, really.

'There are two cottages side by side. Josh, who looks after the cellar door, lives in the other one. He usually heads into town to eat so you'll be able to catch a ride with him if you want.' Be damned if she was going to be expected to play chauffeur.

'If there's a bed, I might just settle for that.'

She glanced across at him, seeing lit up in the headlights of a passing car the weariness that hovered around his eyes and weighed down on his eyelids. 'Worn out after a long day travelling in first class? You have my sympathy. It must be hell.'

'I'm surprised you'd give me the time of day, let alone your sympathy.'

She snorted and manoeuvred the car around a bend. 'Yeah, you're right. You don't have my sympathy.'

Beside her she sensed the shift in his body as he angled himself on the seat. She sensed his eyes on her, and could almost feel the curve of his lips in a smile. She didn't dare look, keeping her eyes on the road ahead instead, but she could feel him watching her and she waited, her heart thumping. She didn't know much about this man, but she'd figured enough to know he wouldn't let her have the last word. 'You don't like me,' he said.

She shifted the gears down before turning into the cottage car park and pulling up in the space outside, ratcheting up the stiff hand brake, thinking about his words and their delivery. He'd made it sound like a challenge, like he was calling her on it, daring her to agree or to back down making excuses.

She wasn't about to back down.

'Don't take it personally.'

'No? How am I supposed to take it?'

She shrugged. 'As a fact of life,' she said, swinging open her door. She found a smile then and turned. 'Like breathing. It just happens.' And then she jumped out.

She didn't wait for him. She grabbed the basket from the back seat and marched up the pathway, searching in her pocket for the key. If she had a choice, she'd hand over the key and leave him to it, but there was a crotchety water heater to turn on that had a degree of difficulty of three-point-five. There was no point even trying to explain it. He'd never fit under the bed anyway, where the damn thing was located.

So she let herself in and snapped on lights and then a gas heater as she went. It was cold inside the small cottage, although the vibe was cosy and embracing. It was decorated for the period, with overstuffed chairs and ruffled curtains and character in every nook and cranny, and Holly loved it. When she'd been a kid, before they'd done it up, she'd used it as her cubby house and her bolt hole. Strange to remember that now, she thought as she shivered. 'It'll soon warm up,' she flung over her shoulder as she bustled through the kitchen, dropping the basket on the small table. 'Have a look around, I just have to turn on the hot water and then it's all yours.'

She looked over her shoulder, satisfied when she saw him prowling around the sitting room, picking up a magazine from the table. Excellent. If she was really quick, she'd be out of there before he realised what she was doing. And the sooner she got the hot water service turned on, the sooner she'd be back in the car and on her way home and maybe then she might be able to relax for ten minutes.

Just as soon as she got this hot water system switched on...

She dropped down on all fours beside the bed and then even lower before shimmying beneath. The switch had been set right in the middle at the back of the bed, just above the skirting. 'Just for laughs,' the electrician had joked when they'd finally found out where he'd put it and called him on it.

Yeah, it was funny all right.

She squirmed closer to the wall, found the switch, flicked it on and, mission accomplished, started backing out.

The cottage was tiny. Done out in girlie fabrics and filled with sofas loaded with cushions that looked like flowers. So not his thing. He dropped the magazine he'd picked up, a tourist guide that was not his thing either, and headed into the kitchen. He saw the basket where she'd dropped it, and hung his coat on a chair nearby, but Holly was nowhere to be seen. Until he went through another doorway and found her.

Or at least found her bottom half poking out from under the bed, a bottom half that was suddenly wriggling backwards, a bottom lifting once clear of the bed.

An unexpectedly shapely bottom.

And if he'd thought her shapeless polo top had been

hiding secrets beneath, her khaki work pants had clearly been hiding a hell of a lot more.

Fabric pulled tight across the cheeks of her bottom, surprisingly, deliciously tight.

And he found his own pants becoming surprisingly tight in response....

Getting hard over prickly Ms Purman?

The jet lag was getting to him. It had to be.

But her rear end was still there wriggling backwards, a peach wrapped in boring khaki but a peach nonetheless, and the heat was still right there, keeping him hard. Keeping his gaze fixed on her.

He put his hand to his head. He wanted to be in bed. In bed and asleep as opposed to being awake and fantasising about the world's least likely conquest.

'Lost something?' he asked, and the woman hauled herself out in a flurry of movement and the back of her head smacked into the iron frame with a loud thunk.

'Ow!'

And he was sorry he'd said anything. Not because she'd hit her head, but because she'd immediately rocked forward on her knees, her hands cradling the back of her head, poking her bottom even higher, the fabric stretched even tighter, and he had the insane desire to peel those khaki work pants off to see if her behind was anywhere near as perfect as it looked.

If it was any other woman, in any other circumstance, he might even give in to temptation.

But this prickly hostile woman?

He must be mad to even think it.

'I didn't lose anything,' she snarled as finally she rocked upright, using the bed to support her as gingerly she got to her feet, one hand still nursing the crash site as she turned around. 'I was turning on the hot water system.'

'Down there?'

'The electrician thought it would be a funny place to put it.' She winced as her fingers found a tender spot. 'Oh, God, can this day get any worse?'

And he couldn't help but smile as she put voice to her frustration, frustration he'd not only shared, but caused. But then he could afford to smile now, because he'd got what he wanted.

Unlike her.

'Here,' he said, taking her by the shoulders and spinning her around, not really feeling guilty even though he had taken her by surprise. 'Let me see.'

She tensed even before he touched her, but he had her turned around before she could tell him not to. 'Where does it hurt?' he asked, his hands still resting warm and heavy on her shoulders while he waited. While her heart thudded so loud in her chest he must surely hear it.

She pointed, eager to distract him before he felt that crazy drumbeat—'Somewhere there'—and held her breath as she felt the slide of his fingers under her ponytail, searching, probing her skull.

'This has to go,' he said, sliding down her hair tie, the tug of it pulling at her hair and making her scalp tingle.

And her hair fell in a thick curtain around her face as his fingers returned, sliding under the weight of it until her breathing grew shallow.

'Ow,' she said, flinching a little as a fingertip grazed the site, 'just there.'

'Let me see,' he said, parting the hair around the spot, tilting her head in his hands so he could see in the dim light cast by the fringed light shade.

She didn't dare breathe. It was enough to feel. It was enough to trace the path of nerves connecting with nerves until she tingled from her head down to her toes and all the places in between. And she wondered about the touch of a man who could make her feel so much with just his fingers to her scalp—and how it would feel if he slid those fingers anywhere near the places where she really tingled—over the nub of her rock-hard nipples, or near the pulsing heat between her thighs.

'It's only a graze but you're going to have a bump,' he said, and she stirred, his breath puffing at her hair, and that sent a new wave of sensation rolling through her, pooling down low and hot in the pit of her belly. 'You might want to ice that when you get back.'

And suddenly his hands were gone and she swayed backwards before she remembered.

Oh, yes. 'Back,' as in home, where she'd been in such a rush to get to a scant minute or two ago, before this man had laced his fingers through her hair and set her scalp alight and made her forget who he was.

A Chatsfield.

A man no doubt used to snapping his fingers and having women line up to share his bed.

And she'd felt his fingers in her hair and imagined...

She had to get out of there! She spun around but he was still there. Instead of being right behind her though, now he was right in front of her and she was trapped between two walls and a bed and a man that stood between her and freedom and so she did the only thing she could do.

She snapped.

'So now you're a doctor?'

Those cool grey eyes merely blinked down at her before he shook his head and sat down on the bed. Which would have been fine except his damned legs were so long she was still trapped. 'What?' he said, reefing off first one and then the other of his expensive shoes.

'As well as being an heir to a hotel fortune and Italian vineyard owner, I mean.'

His socks followed. 'Your point being?'

'It's just you seem to like dribbling out the details, making us think one thing while all the while something else is true.'

'I didn't make you think one thing—you decided I knew nothing about wine all by yourself.' He put his hands to the band of his knitted top and, before she realised what he was doing, reefed it over his head, tossing it into a corner.

Panic squeezed her lungs. 'What are you doing?'

'I'm getting undressed. You can stay and argue if you want, but I'm going to bed.' He stood, bare-chested, his skin gleaming olive in the thin light, and put his hand to his trousers and suddenly she didn't care how much space he took up, she was going to get around him and through that door.

'I'm leaving,' she said, practically hugging the wall to get past. But she turned at the door, keeping her eyes firmly fixed on a wall so there was no chance she would witness if he did drop his trousers before she got the last word in. 'Oh, and I was wrong before and you were right.'

He sighed. 'I don't get you.'

'I don't like you,' she said over her shoulder, 'and it *is* personal.'

Yesterday's storms had long gone, the morning mist hanging like veils between the gums, swirling damp kisses to her cheeks as she worked, snippers in her hand cutting the new shoots off at the second bud. Some days she'd find the odd kangaroo or two grazing near where she worked, or there would be a brand-new lamb arrived overnight to welcome her.

She loved this season in the vineyard, a time she could

be at one with the vines, talking to them, whispering words of encouragement as she went.

And she loved this time of the day.

Usually.

Not today.

Today there were no kangaroos and no brand-new lambs to make her smile. Today there were mutters instead of whispers. Today there were kookaburras laughing in the gum trees. Today her gut was wound tighter than a vine on a wire.

Because today Franco was joining her with the pruning.

The snippers in her hand felt awkward and uncoop-erative and not for the first time she glanced down at her watch. Not for the first time she asked herself why she bothered checking. It was still early and they would be hours yet. Apparently Josh had taken Franco into town to the menswear supplier and no doubt a decent breakfast while they were waiting for the shops to open.

Thank God for Josh. She didn't want to be the one today to knock on Franco's door and rouse him if he was still sleeping. She didn't want to risk a second look at that bare chest or see his long wavy hair tousled by sleep or his square chin adorned in designer stubble.

She didn't even want to think about that bare chest and all that olive skin or the tone of the muscles packed be-neath. Neither did she want to remember the feel of his hands in her hair and on her scalp and what his touch had done to the rest of her.

No, the only thing she wanted was to see the back of him. And fully clothed into the deal.

She snipped her way along the row, some measure of an-ticipation fizzing in her blood. Today was the test. Franco had told them he could prune. He'd agreed that if he was rubbish, the deal was off. Today they'd get to find out if he'd spoken the truth or whether he'd overplayed his hand.

And whether she could breathe again without the risk of breathing air flavoured by him.

The tightness in her gut pulled another notch tighter. But given how confident he'd been of his talents, how much chance was there of that happening any time soon?

She heard them before she saw them. Two men talking somewhere out there in the mist in low tones, one voice unmistakably Australian, the other a blend, a product of two foreign cultures.

And their voices were like two different varieties of wine, she mused, two different characters with different top and bottom notes and regional flavours.

They were laughing at a shared joke, loud and uncontained, and for one horrible moment Holly had the feeling they were laughing about her.

She'd given Franco enough ammunition for a few good jokes. Had he shared the story of her fleeing from his bedroom as he'd got undressed?

And she was just telling herself not to be so paranoid when she saw them emerge from the swirling mist and they saw her and they both stopped laughing and she felt even sicker.

Josh waved. Franco kept his hands in his pockets.

At least she assumed it must be Franco, except he looked more like something out of an RM Williams bush outfitters ad, all decked out in slim-fitting moleskin jeans and boots and a dark jacket and with an Akubra on his head and all brand-spanking-new.

He could have looked ridiculous.

Knowing who he was, he should have looked ridiculous. He was no more stockman or station worker than Father Christmas.

Instead he looked amazing as he walked towards her, like a male model walking out of a magazine, his expression unreadable, all long-limbed and relaxed in his own skin.

But then she'd seen that skin and he had every reason to be relaxed.

She swallowed, and warned herself not to go there.

'Holly!' Josh called as the pair drew closer. 'Look what I found. Reckon he could almost pass for a local. Whaddayareckon?'

Holly reckoned Franco looked even better close up. Close up she could see just how well those moleskin jeans fitted legs more used to wearing fine Italian fabrics. There was a check shirt under that jacket and a leather belt and buckle and, damn the man to hell and back, but the look suited him and suited him well. And close up she could see the shadowed face under the brim of his hat and could see it was even more Chatsfield-esquely beautiful than she remembered. Not that she was about to admit any of that. She smiled. At least she hoped it was a smile rather than a leer. 'He sure could pass for a local, Josh, at least until he opens his mouth.'

Franco didn't.

He was too busy remembering how Holly had looked last night with her hair down. He'd pulled off her elastic to check out her head wound not thinking it would make any great difference, but then she'd turned and looked up at him with those big blue eyes, and honey-blonde hair had framed her face and kissed her shoulders, and for a moment he'd been speechless.

Jet lag couldn't be responsible for everything, he'd figured, but with her big blue eyes and her hair around her face, the woman had looked halfway edible.

Whereas today it was scraped right back again, almost as if she was punishing it. Good.

Which reminded him...

'Good morning, Holly,' he said in an impeccable tone. 'I have something of yours.' She blinked up at him, confusion muddying her blue eyes. 'You left it in the cottage last night.'

He placed something feather-light in the palm of her hand. She looked down to see a black circle of elastic and her stomach clenched. Her hair tie.

She reddened as her fingers curled around it and she realised Josh was looking on. It would hardly help to say she hadn't left it so much as he hadn't given it back to her. It would hardly help at all.

'Thanks very much,' she said through gritted teeth as she shoved the offending article into a pocket in her jacket.

'My pleasure,' he said with a shrug. 'So where do I start?'

She sent him off towards a bucket containing gloves and snips at the end of the row.

Josh watched him, scratching his head. 'So...you got a thing for Franco?'

Holly watched him too, liking altogether too much the way the man looked from behind as he strode across the earth. 'Yeah, I've got a thing for Franco, all right. Right now, I'd like to kill him.'

CHAPTER FIVE

'WHY DID YOU do that?' she demanded the minute Josh had disappeared. 'You know what Josh is thinking now.'

'What's Josh thinking now?'

'That I spent time in your cottage last night.'

'You did.'

'But not because of that!'

He rubbed his brow. 'Is that supposed to be a euphemism for you willingly spending the night in my bed?'

'You know damn well it is!'

'So you want me to tell Josh we didn't sleep together?'

'No! I don't want you telling Josh anything!'

'So you want him to think we're sleeping together?'

'*No!* Just forget I said anything!' She took a deep breath, pulled on a pair of gloves and said, 'Right, now, this is the way we do it here.'

He listened to her with a wry smile on his face. He didn't care one way or another whether she was sleeping with the hired help. He just wanted to know if she was. You never knew when something like that might come in handy.

He'd told her he knew how to prune, but Holly still gave him a lesson in it anyway. She didn't know how they did it in Italy, but she sure as hell wasn't trusting her vines to anyone without explaining the way she expected it done. Even if he considered himself some kind of expert.

And then they'd started either side of the row together, snipping at the shoots, cutting off everything after the second bud, so she could keep a watchful eye on him. If he was going to be lousy at the job, he'd soon know about it and he'd be on the next plane back.

He was pruning the vines at the right place, she acceded, but he was painstakingly slow. She slowed her own pace down so much it was painful when she could have been quarter way along the row by now.

She whispered an apology to the vines as he dropped the snips. 'Something wrong?' she asked him.

'They slipped,' he said, and she smiled.

Game on.

Already her mind was ticking over—how long should she give him? How much time before the inevitable happened and he had to admit defeat? Because if the pruning was going to take this long, she might as well do it herself.

He dropped the snips again and cursed.

'Having trouble?'

'I'm out of practice, that's all.'

'Let me know if you want to give up. I won't hold it against you.'

'Not a chance,' he growled, and started snipping in earnest.

And before long she didn't have to hold herself back. She was easing off the brake, keeping up with his newly acquired pace, matching it and then matching it as he ratcheted up the pace again. She kept a close eye on what he was doing, looking for shortcuts he was taking, searching for faults, but his work looked faultless, as sure and as certain as her own.

Damn.

By morning teatime they'd completed the first two rows

together. They dropped the snips into a bucket and spread out on a mat Josh had delivered with a basket Gus had prepared for them. The mist had cleared from the trees and now the air was cool and sharp, under a thin blue sky almost cloud free, and Holly was considering how she was going to spend the next six weeks with this man by her side, knowing he could do the job he'd promised to do, knowing what that meant for the future of Purman Wines.

The deal might have already been done and dusted and Franco long gone.

And now all she had to hope for was another Chatsfield scandal.

Not too much to ask for, certainly not too much to expect, but the way her luck seemed to be running lately...

'What's wrong with your grandfather?' asked Franco, interrupting her thoughts as he took a bite from a slab of cake after Josh had disappeared.

She blinked and looked over at him. 'Pardon?'

'The wheelchair,' he said. 'Why does he need it?'

'Pop had an accident on an all-terrain bike,' she said, 'a four-wheeler. He hit a depression and it flipped and pinned him by the hip. He was lucky, as it happens.'

Hesitation. 'And he'll be okay?'

She looked at him suspiciously. 'What are you worried about? That your precious contract could blow up in your face if something happened to Pop?'

'Maybe I was just asking after his welfare.'

And she felt shamed that she had jumped down his throat and wondered what it was about this man that put her hackles up. She nursed her coffee in her hands and blew on the surface. 'He'll be as good as new, so long as he does his exercises. He'll be walking before harvest.'

'Why isn't Josh helping with the pruning?'

'He doesn't like to. Reckons he's all thumbs.' She

shrugged. 'Lost the tips of a couple of fingers once so I can understand he's not keen. But he's a whiz in the cellar door, as well as managing the sheep we use to keep the grass down in winter.'

'So, how am I doing. Am I a "whiz" in the vines?'

She poured more coffee from the thermos and surveyed him under her lashes. He was propped up on one elbow on the waterproof rug like he owned it, long and lean in his moleskins and oh-so-relaxed. He knew damned well how he was doing. 'I've seen worse,' she conceded, and curse him to hell and back, he chuckled as she handed him his mug.

Curse him to hell and back, she liked the sound, even if she knew he was laughing at her.

'High praise,' he said as he took off his new Akubra with his free hand and dropped it on the ground, raking through his hair with his fingers.

Her own scalp tingled at the sight. She knew how those fingers felt in her hair—like a caress against her scalp. She sipped her coffee, wondering again how good they would feel against her skin. Hating herself for going there.

'Holly?'

Her coffee cup lingered at her lips. 'Hmm?'

'I asked you a question.'

'Oh. Sorry,' she said, hoping the heat in her cheeks didn't betray just what she'd been so absorbed thinking about. This man would just love to know that. Not. It was hardly the kind of thing she wanted to admit even to herself. She didn't even like the man and now she was fantasising about how his fingers would feel on her skin.

Madness!

'I couldn't help but notice…' He hesitated. 'You talk to yourself a lot as you work.'

'No, I don't.'

'I heard you. You talk. A lot.'

'I'm not talking to myself.'

'No?'

'No. I'm talking to the vines.'

'You talk to the vines?'

She shrugged, her blue eyes intent on him, flashing out a challenge. Was he calling her weird? 'Sure I do. Something wrong with that?'

'What do you talk about?' he said, the corners of his lips twitching like he thought it was the funniest thing he'd ever heard but he was too polite to laugh out loud. 'The weather?'

'Sometimes,' she said, deadpan. She was good at what she did. She didn't have to defend herself or her methods, however unconventional, to anyone. 'I've known these vines all my life. They're like old friends. And like old friends, they like to hear if they're looking good, and at other times they need a word of encouragement or two.' She raised her chin. 'What's so hard to understand about that?'

His eyes narrowed. 'So is that why they call you the wine whisperer, because you actually talk to the vines?'

She pulled a face as she tossed the dregs of her coffee onto the grass and stacked the empty cup in the basket.

She didn't have to explain anything to him.

She was still cranky about him proving to be such an excellent pruner.

She was even more cranky thinking that the way he was going, sooner or later he might even beat her up a row, and wasn't that going to sting!

She didn't want to think about how cranky it made her that she'd actually enjoyed this break.

'Isn't that just the dumbest name?' she said, standing up and brushing imaginary grass from her trousers and putting a full stop on the conversation. 'We should get back to work.'

CHAPTER SIX

THEY'D PRUNED FOR two and a half days straight and her back knew it and her neck knew it. At the end of a row she straightened to stretch the kinks out of her spine while she rubbed her neck and looked at her watch. Good timing. If she stopped now she'd have just enough time to get showered and grab a bite to eat before she needed to head off to her appointment down at Port MacDonnell. She was looking forward to the trip. If nothing else, it would give her a few welcome daylight hours' respite from the man who'd been shadowing her along the rows.

Two and a half straight days and she felt like she'd been through the emotional wringer. First had come the anger that Franco had arrived expecting to waltz in and waltz out on the next plane with the rights to their next vintage tied in a big red bow. How many times that day had she thought she'd prevailed and that Franco would soon be on his way?

Wrongly, as it turned out. Because she'd been cornered—blackmailed, really—into a deal at the last moment, with only the glimmer of hope that his claims to pruning were overblown to buoy her.

That glimmer had been extinguished the first morning, so then had followed the dull grey blanket of resignation, the knowledge that any hopes of an early escape from this deal were gone.

She felt like a woman who'd fallen overboard and was waiting for a lifeline.

That lifeline now rested with someone in his family tripping up on the world stage in the next few weeks.

It shouldn't be a big ask. It really shouldn't. They were Chatsfields after all. It was in their DNA to mess up. Hadn't the youngest one, Cara, been in the news lately—something about a card game in Las Vegas? Surely she couldn't stay out of trouble for too long?

And yet the knowledge that she was going to be scouring the web every night looking for a story—a scandal—that would save Purman Wines from the clutches of Chatsfield Hotels seemed a pretty shabby kind of lifeline.

But it was all she had.

That and the promise of a few hours away from the man who had caused all this trouble in the first place.

And right now the promise of those few hours was like a beacon.

'Lunchtime!' she called, wondering where the hell Franco had got to, given they'd started at the same time. She caught a glimpse of movement but it was a couple of rows on and finally she found reason for a smile. They'd agreed to do alternate rows and clearly he'd started on the wrong one.

Not such an expert after all.

'You missed a row,' she called when he looked up, and he scowled and shook his head and for a second she assumed he hadn't heard her, until she took a few steps closer and realised that the row she was accusing him of missing was pruned as neatly as one of her own.

'How did you do that?' she asked, not a little bit peeved, as he came closer, pulling off his gloves.

'Simple. I don't waste time communing with the assets.'

'I'll have you know it's not wasting time, Mr Chatsfield.'

'And I'll have you know I was teasing, Ms Purman. I told you I'd done this before. I just took some time getting into my stride.'

And she could see he was laughing because his grey eyes were creased at the corners and his lips were twitching, but before she could tell him she didn't think it was very funny—and how could she? She was still stinging from discovering her student was truly a gun pruner—her mobile buzzed in her pocket. 'Pop,' she said turning away, 'I was just about to head back—

'You're kidding,' she said a moment later, glancing again quickly at her watch. 'Okay, let them know I'll be there in an hour.'

'That's it for the day,' she said as she swung around, gathering up snips and gloves in a bucket.

'Already? It's still early.'

'I've got an appointment down at Port MacDonnell. A wine order to finesse for a wedding happening next weekend. Only they've brought it forward to lunchtime so both bride and groom can be there.'

'They couldn't just phone an order in?'

'They want at least ten dozen of our best sparkling, recently disgorged, and that's just for the toasts. No, Franco, they could not just call it in. That's not the way we operate.'

'Fine. You go then. But I can't see any need for me to stop.'

Did he really think she was going to let him loose on her vines without her being around? Besides, what was wrong with him? The man had arrived after twenty-four-plus hours in the air and been thrown the very next day into laborious physical work. What was he trying to prove?

Rhetorical question. She knew exactly what he was trying to prove.

'You really don't have to try to prove that you're better than your average Chatsfield, you know. You're not going to impress anybody with those tactics, least of all me, so there's no point. And anyway, you've got the deal you wanted, so why not just take the afternoon off and celebrate?'

His eyes narrowed and she wondered what nerve she'd hit. Then again, with a family like his, he'd probably have a few raw ends rattling around. She was bound to hit one sooner or later.

'The deal was six weeks' work. I'm here to work.'

'So go help Josh in the cellar door if you like. Friday afternoons can be busy with early weekend traffic. But maybe Gus has a better idea.'

Gus didn't. His idea was much, much worse. 'Why not take Franco with you to the Port?' he said. 'You can show him Mount Gambier's Blue Lake on the way.'

'We won't have time on the way.'

'So show him on the way back.'

'I thought Franco could help Josh in the cellar door.'

'Josh'll be just fine.'

'But Franco could learn the ropes. He is here to work. No passengers, remember?'

Gus raised his hands in the air in question. 'Since when has visiting clients not been work?'

And it would have been churlish for Holly to keep arguing even if she could think of another argument, but suddenly she could see her Franco-free afternoon evaporating as completely as the morning mist hanging between the trees had done.

'Fine,' she huffed as she headed for her bedroom for a quick freshen up. 'He can come.'

* * *

'I'll drive,' Franco offered.

She regarded him suspiciously, remembering the last time she'd driven him. 'I don't always kangaroo hop at the start, if that's what you're worried about.'

He smiled and she found herself wishing he wouldn't do that. It was much easier to remember not to like him when he didn't smile. It was much easier to be at war when there could be no peace. 'I like driving. It'll be a change to drive on the right side of the road.'

'We drive on the left side here,' she warned before she let go of the keys into his hand, wondering afresh if she was doing the right thing.

His smile widened. 'Like I said, the right side.'

And too late she realised what he'd meant all along and what she should have clicked to straightaway except that it was him and that he tied her so far up in knots that she couldn't think straight. She clambered up into the high passenger seat feeling a beat behind, and not just because he'd been burning up the rows faster than she had.

The highway to Penola was long and straight and lined either side with vines and she'd seen it all before many times anyway. So was it any wonder that her eyes were drawn to the way his hands worked the steering wheel and gearstick instead?

Good hands, she decided, long-fingered hands that could wield a mean pair of snips one minute and caress a cranky old four-wheel drive into submission the next.

She looked out of her window as they passed block after block of vines and sighed and wished those hands belonged to somebody else.

Anybody else.

'It's flat here,' he said as they drove down the highway.

It was the first thing he'd said and Holly swung her head around. 'It is around here. What's it like in Italy?'

He shrugged. 'Different.'

'Like, it has hills?'

'Yes.'

Great, she thought, so much for conversation. And she wondered if she'd imagined it. She looked out the window again. Looked back. 'So what made you go to Italy when all your family are in England?'

'My mother is Italian,' he answered with a shrug.

'Do you live near her?'

There was a pause that she sensed was weighted with meaning. And then he asked, 'How far is it to Port MacDonnell again?'

The township of Penola was long behind them, the road more windy. She could have sat there enjoying the scenery, but while the view was pretty, it gave her time to think about other things, and the one thing that dominated her mind was Franco.

His scent filled her every breath. His proximity alerted her every moment. Silence was no respite. He didn't have to talk for her to know he was right there, alongside her, no matter how hard she studied the view.

In which case there was no reason she shouldn't ask the questions she wanted to ask. 'So why did you move to Italy?'

He spared her but a glance before checking his mirrors. 'It seemed like the right thing to do at the time.'

'And,' she ventured warily, 'was it?'

'It was,' he said, indicating to overtake a car towing a horse float. 'The absolute right thing.'

'Do you see much of your family?'

'Not much.'

'That's a shame.'

'Is it? I thought you were the one who believed my family was good for nothing more than magazine fodder.'

And it shamed her into silence that he was right.

The road was quiet and they made good time, so good that they did have time to check out the Blue Lake on the way.

'Do you want to stop?' she asked.

'I thought we didn't have time,' he said, and she knew he'd known she hadn't wanted him along.

'There was less traffic than I expected.'

Franco just smiled that knowing smile again and she hated that he seemed able to peel away her words and see into her mind. They walked to the lookout at the crater's edge, where the bush-covered walls of the crater fell steeply away to the lake below.

'It doesn't look very blue,' he said, peering down at the steel-grey waters.

'It never does this time of year. It's this steel-grey colour from about April to November. But if you were here in December you'd see it turn a vivid blue, almost overnight it seems to happen.'

He looked down at the cold grey lake below them and then over at her. 'As blue as your eyes?'

She blinked, clamping down on a zipper line of sensation that shimmied down her spine and left her tingling in all sorts of places she didn't realise could tingle. Strange, she thought, when all he'd done was notice her eyes were blue. 'Much deeper,' she said, unimpressed with the little tremor that rattled through her words. She licked her lips and tried for steadier this time. 'More a cobalt or a sapphire-blue.'

'Whereas yours are what?' He took his own good time studying them, although if she wasn't mistaken, those eyes had also spent a goodly amount of time examining her mouth. 'What would you call them? Turquoise?'

She shrugged and turned away, feeling a little bit thrown, a little bit off balance. 'I guess.' She pointed out an old stone building, eager to happen upon a diversion, eager to change the subject. 'Over there is the old pumping station. It's not in operation any more,' she babbled, 'even though Mount Gambier still takes its water from the lake.'

He nodded and for a moment she imagined she was home free. 'And what's that?' he said, referring to the abandoned ruins across from the lookout on the crater edge.

'Ah,' she answered a little wistfully, sad to be reminded of the wreck it had been allowed to become, a connection to her earliest days now just a derelict eyesore surrounded by chain-link fence. 'That's the old hospital.'

Although it could never just be the 'old hospital' to her, because she knew her father had once walked those hallways treating his patients and her mother had given birth to her in a room overlooking the lake. And in the end, that's where they'd both been taken after the crash that had claimed their lives.

But now only the shell of that building remained in place of memories, and even across the crater's rim, she could sense the wind whistle and moan through the shattered windows and up the empty stairwells, giving voice to the ghosts of the past.

She shivered.

He sensed her sadness, not just in the way she said the words, but in her utter stillness, her turquoise eyes fixed but unseeing across the crater, as if every part of her was holding something tightly bound inside.

And then she seemed to sense him watching her, sense him wondering, and she shivered and whatever spell she was under was broken. 'I was born there,' she said briskly. Then she shook her head and let the wind peel back the loose strands of her hair from her face as she turned towards the car. 'We'd better get going if we're going to get to this meeting on time.'

Thirty kilometres farther through green pastured land sat the coastal town of Port MacDonnell, a sleepy fishing and holiday village now, where a century ago it had been a bustling port.

Right on the esplanade stood a grand old double-storey stone building overlooking the jetty that had once served as the Customs House. A German mine from World War II that had washed ashore on the beach sat in pride of place on the front lawn. 'The wedding is to be held in the local church but the reception will be here. I just have to work out a few details for the order. Why don't you take a walk out along the shore? I won't be too long.'

'Given I'm supposed to be working, I'd prefer to tag along.' He was curious to see her operate away from her beloved vines, and dealing with customers one on one. From what he'd heard the few times he'd visited the town, a kind of folklore had built up around Holly Purman, and as far as the locals were concerned, it seemed she could do no wrong. 'I'd like to see how you deal with customers who are lucky enough not to be cursed with the Chatsfield name.'

She drew her shoulders up at that, no apology to be seen in eyes the colour of glacial meltwaters, more a note of resignation. 'Suit yourself.'

Inside the building the happy couple was already busy with the function manager comparing lists and making notes, and the next sixty minutes were spent considering menu choices and matching them with wines.

An hour later, Franco had to admit that Holly was more

than good at what she did. She had a passion about her wines that she brought with her—a passion that shone right through those boring khaki work clothes.

Yet more boring khaki work clothes.

And he wondered as he watched her—given she'd changed before they'd started out—did she ever wear anything else other than her polo shirts, work pants and boots? Anything else that made something of the curves he knew she had hidden away under those oh-so-practical layers?

If he had to sum up her wardrobe in two words, it would be *designerless drab*. And if he could nominate one area where she had no gut instinct at all, this was the one.

Because otherwise, whether out in the cold morning air whispering to her vines, or dealing with clients face-to-face, she was supreme. Today she had listened to what everyone had to say, paying special heed to how the bride and groom wanted their wedding to be. She'd made suggestions when there were none forthcoming. She'd sorted out problems that were foreseen and made provision for uncertainties and things that might go wrong.

And she'd smiled.

And that smile and those eyes were a killer combination. It made everyone in the room feel good.

Including him.

And that was the biggest revelation of them all.

An hour later the order was complete and they were heading back to the car when he saw the sign for the takeaway shop down the road. His stomach rumbled and he remembered they'd missed lunch in the rush to get away.

'Why don't we grab something to eat while we're here?'

She followed the direction he was looking and asked, 'Fish and chips?'

And after more than a dozen years living in Italy, the very idea of fish and chips sounded exotic. 'Why not?'

So they bought fish and chips with wedges of lemon all wrapped in paper from the café and found a bench overlooking the rocky beach to the marina and breakwater beyond.

The sun was warm when it peeked out from behind the odd cloud, the wind too lazy today to neutralise the effect, and the fish and chips were so good they were content to just sit and eat and watch the fishing boats bobbing on their lines. How long was it since she'd had the chance to sit and eat fish and chips at the beach? She couldn't remember the last time.

And never in a million years would she have believed it possible today, not with Franco Chatsfield for company.

So maybe her stomach had been rumbling up a storm and the smell of frying fish and salty chips had been too much to resist, but still she wondered what kind of seismic shift had occurred that they could sit like this so companionably together.

'That was good,' he said on a sigh, screwing up his paper in his hands and leaning back, hooking his elbows over the back of the seat and stretching out his long legs in front of him.

She tried not to notice. She did her best to ignore the hand resting lazily just inches from her shoulder and to focus on what was left of her fish. She did her best to look at the boats. The birds. The clouds. But, God, his legs looked so good in moleskins and boots it was hard to stay focused on anything else.

The young girl serving in the fish and chip shop hadn't looked for distractions, even before he'd opened his mouth and that unique mix of English/Continental accent had emerged and she'd all but swooned. With his long wavy hair and drop dead gorgeous looks, the girl had stared at him like one might admire some kind of exotic butterfly that had somehow accidentally fluttered into your orbit, and Franco hadn't seemed to either notice or mind the open adoration one little bit.

She wiped her hands and stretched out Franco-like on the seat and realised she envied the fish and chip shop girl.

Because it wouldn't be half bad not to know or mind that he was a Chatsfield.

It wouldn't be half bad not to have to care.

And then you could just concentrate on his good looks and his sexy voice and the way he turned the contents of a bush outfitters catalogue into sex on legs and then the rest of it wouldn't matter.

She might even like the man then.

She might even find herself wanting to share a park bench with him.

But he was a Chatsfield and she had to care.

Still, it was nice sitting here overlooking a beach and feeling impossibly full in the thin sunshine even if it was with him. She'd just never figured him for a man who might possibly enjoy the simpler things in life.

'You know,' she started cautiously, still looking out to sea because it was much easier talking to the shifting sea than looking him in the eyes, 'I never figured you for a fish-and-chips-wrapped-in-paper-at-the-beach kind of man.'

'No?' he said, sounding as relaxed and content as she felt. 'What kind of man did you figure me for?'

'Lobster and caviar. Truffles and foie gras. Maybe a gamey meat with some kind of fancy sauce—not too much, mind, just enough to be drizzled artistically around the plate.'

'Why would you think that?'

'Because you're a—' she stopped herself just short '—so wealthy.'

'Because I'm a Chatsfield,' he said, and she could just about hear the smile in his voice. 'That's what you were about to say.'

Holly screwed up her nose. She hated it that he was right. She hated that he made it sound so unjust on her part. But he didn't sound angry or even accusatory, just stating a fact, so maybe he really was enjoying the same post-fish-and-chips glow that she was. 'Same thing, really.'

'We get special dispensation, of course.'

'For what?'

'From eating all that lobster and gamey meat with fancy sauce all the time. It's written into the Chatsfield family rules. We're allowed one day off a month to slum it like normal mortals.'

And she couldn't help it. She laughed, his reply as unexpected as the discovery he had a sense of humour. 'Then you're in big trouble, Franco. Because corned beef sandwiches aren't exactly haute cuisine.'

'There goes the inheritance,' he said with a wistful sigh. 'Easy come, easy go.'

If they'd been on good terms from the start—friendly terms—she would have laughed some more.

But they hadn't been on good terms ever—so maybe there really was something in the combination of fresh fish and crunchy chips at a winter beach blessed with the sun that gave her the courage not to laugh, but to hesitate a moment and ask, 'Why are you being so nice?'

'Am I? I just see two people sitting on a bench, talking.'

'But one of those people is me, and I haven't been entirely welcoming.'

She caught his shrug out of the corner of her eye. 'You

have your reasons. Maybe over the time I'm here, you might feel differently.'

She shook her head, suddenly weighed down by the reality of the situation again. The impossibility of the situation.

'I'm sorry, I don't see how that's possible. I mean, I know that it's almost inevitable that once the pruning is completed, you're going to get those signatures on the contract that you wanted. But how can I forget all those stories I've read? How can I trust that Purman Wines won't be dragged into such a scandal or merely charged as guilty by association?'

'Those stories you might read while at the dentist, you mean? The ones that show my family in all its faded glory, parading themselves shamelessly in front of the media every scandal-ridden chance they get?'

Now she was looking at him, the sea and the boats forgotten. Something about the way he'd said those words alerted her that maybe he wasn't so proud of his family's media coverage after all.

She nodded. 'Yeah, those stories.'

He turned his grey eyes upon hers. 'And the ones you've tarred me with, using the same brush.'

'Well...' And she wavered, thinking back, remembering those articles and searching her memory for any that featured Franco—there must have been at least one—and she looked back at him and was immediately rewarded with the sight of him and his film-star looks with his long limbs stretched out easily as if he were staking a claim, and she was glad he looked as good as sin, because it flashed warning lights that reinforced the whole Chatsfield brand loud and clear.

Entitled. Flashy. Trashy.

And even if that assessment sat uncomfortably with

what she'd seen of Franco and his work ethic in the past couple of days—still he was part of that same tribe, and part of the biggest stumbling block she had against this deal. How could he not see that? How could she make it plain?

'You're still a Chatsfield, aren't you?'

A frown tugged at the skin between his eyebrows. 'Ouch. That hurts.'

'That's what I say when I'm at the dentist.'

'Maybe you should ask for pain relief.'

And she wasn't sure if they were still talking about the same thing any more or whether they were talking cross-purposes, but pain was something she knew about.

Pain was something she'd experienced and survived.

'I think pain can be good, if it teaches you not to do stupid things.'

If it reminds you not to go there again.

Like a niggling voice was reminding her now.

'So you still believe doing this deal with Chatsfield would be stupid?'

She tilted her head towards the sea, watching the boats tugging back and forth on their moorings, thinking how strange it was to discuss these issues without heat or rancour. But what point was heat or rancour now when the deal had been struck and it was up to Franco to fulfil his end before they would sign?

'At the very least it would be reckless. We're a young business, if not in years of operation, then in terms of our success. It wouldn't take much to shake the industry's confidence in us and lose the goodwill we've built up.'

'Reckless doesn't always have to be negative. Reckless can be exciting. Sometimes you just have to take a risk. A leap of faith if you like.'

'Not if you're dicing with your entire business, you

don't. Because then reckless becomes dangerous, maybe even borders on irresponsible. No, I'm sorry, but there's no way I can ever believe this is a good deal for Purman Wines.' She stopped herself then. 'Damn. And you were being so nice.'

'It wouldn't have lasted,' he said, and if his unexpected humour had surprised her, he surprised her even more when he hauled her up by one hand. 'Come on. Let's go for a walk.'

CHAPTER SEVEN

HOLLY HAD NEVER liked jetties. It was crazy. She knew it was. She'd lived in the Coonawarra all her life and this was as close to a local beach as the district had and she loved the coast, but there was something about the creaking timbers and the cracks between where you could see the sea surging and foaming below that she'd never felt comfortable walking out on a groaning timber platform. It felt uncomfortably like the ground was constantly shifting beneath her feet.

She didn't like the ground shifting beneath her feet.

And every now and then there would be a patch of new timbers, where the old rotten beams had been replaced, but always in a patch, and she'd always wondered how they'd worked out that those timbers needed to be replaced or whether they'd waited for someone to fall through first.

She avoided the old worn beams where she could. She didn't want to be the reason for the next batch of running repairs.

But she wasn't about to admit that to Franco. Stoically she shoved her hands in her jacket, and not just because she was afraid he might grab her hand again anytime soon. She kept her eyes on her feet and where they were placed, favouring the newer beams, or finding a path along where timbers had been bolted onto supporting beams below, avoiding anywhere where the gap between timbers was more than a centimetre.

And staying right away from the side that had no safety fence. Right away.

And while she was conscious of every nail-biting step, Franco meanwhile was oblivious to the dangers, maybe because his feet were so big there was no way he could fall between the cracks, or maybe because he knew no jetty in its right mind would dare dump a Chatsfield into the briny depths.

A beam creaked and gave a little under her foot and a stomach full of fish and chips flipped over.

A stomach that didn't right itself until they'd reached the end of the jetty and the handrail she could cling to while she took a few calming breaths.

Franco made small talk with a couple of the locals dangling lines over the side, asking if they'd caught anything and checking out the fish they were proud to show off.

Holly wasn't interested in the catch of the day. She turned her face into the wind and breathed in the salt-kissed air, knowing that for at least a minute or two she was safe. She closed her eyes and sucked in air and let the calls of the gulls remind her she was still alive while the blustery wind at the end of the jetty buffeted her worried brow.

She could do this.

She was wound up tighter than a fisherman's reel. He'd put her lack of conversation on the way out here down to her still feeling uncomfortable about the way that last discussion had gone, but right now she looked ill as she clung white knuckled to the handrail.

He put one hand to her shoulder. 'Are you okay?' Her shoulder jerked back as her eyes flew open. Turquoise eyes spiked with fear.

'I'm fine.'

'Are you?'

A moment's hesitation. That pink tip of tongue flicking at her lips once more. Before teeth nibbling at her lips gave way to a weak smile. 'Of course I am.'

'You don't look fine.'

Her eyes looked everywhere but at him. 'Okay. So maybe I'm not a big fan of jetties,' she confessed. 'That's all.'

'You what?'

'I don't like the gaps and how you can see the sea moving underneath and the creaking timbers and the rusting bolts and the feeling that if I drop something it'll tumble into the ocean and I'll never see it again.' She paused, breathless, her turquoise eyes beseeching, begging for his understanding.

'Can't you swim? Is that what you're afraid of?'

'Of course I can swim! It's this thing, creaking and shifting. I don't like it, that's all.'

'Do you want to go back?'

Her eyes flared with fear. One hand flew from her hand-rail long enough to make a stop signal before finding the rail again. 'No! Not just yet. Just give me a minute or two. I'll be fine.'

He hunkered down on the railing alongside her, looking out to the breakwater that blocked the worst of the angry sea to protect the fishing fleet. Who would have thought it? His wine-whispering nemesis and the woman who'd defended her precious wines like a pit bull was afraid of something as simple as a jetty.

'Why did you agree to come out here, if you feel this way? Why didn't you say something?'

'I didn't want you to know.'

'Why not?'

'I didn't want you to think I was pathetic.'

'I don't think you're pathetic.'

'Yeah, right. Fully grown woman afraid of a little beach infrastructure. Nothing pathetic about that. Nothing funny about that.'

'I'm not laughing, Holly.'

She looked at him then, almost as if to check, to examine his eyes for a telltale glimmer of humour before she swung her head back out to sea. It was a full minute before she could bring herself to talk. 'Nan and Pop brought me here once, when I was little. I had my favourite teddy by the hand, swinging it in my hand like Pop was swinging mine. Then there was a sudden gust of wind and the teddy fell free and bounced and skidded over the planks and landed in the sea. And as I watched it float away, I wondered why nobody jumped in to rescue it.'

'Is that when you started not liking jetties?'

'No. I don't think I liked them before. All those gaps between the timbers. All that ocean right there below your feet, sucking at the pilings.' She shivered. 'But that day proved I was right to be wary.'

And because he thought a change of subject might be a good idea and because he wondered, he asked, 'How long have you lived with Gus?'

She shrugged, still looking out to sea. 'Since I was three. Since Mum and Dad were killed in a car crash.'

There was a moment's hesitation. 'I wondered about your parents. I didn't want to ask.'

'It's no secret. And I had Gus and Esme, at least until Esme died. The worst part is not remembering my parents.' He watched as a frown creased her brow. 'You know, I see photographs and I see the hospital ruins where my dad worked—the ruins on the crater by the lake where we stopped on the way...' She watched him, waiting for his nod before she continued. 'And I know they were my parents, but they're almost an abstract concept. Does that make sense? And yet a teddy, I remember the grief I felt at watching my teddy drifting away on the sea like it was the most important thing in the world.'

She turned towards him. 'That's mad, isn't it?'

And she looked up at him, appealing to him with those turquoise eyes and with flushed lips parted in question and the loose ends of her hair flying free around her face and he did the only possible thing he could.

He leaned down and kissed her. No more than a brush of lips against lips, no more than a tasting, a sampling, feather-light and barely there.

But enough to learn she tasted salty and womanly, like he imagined a mermaid would taste, plucked fresh from the sea.

Enough to have her go perfectly rigid at his side. Her tongue flicked at her lips, almost as if checking for evidence. 'Why did you do that?' she asked, her voice husky and raw, her cheeks sucking the heat from her eyes.

He wasn't entirely sure he knew. How did you explain away an impulse? 'Because you looked like a woman who needed a kiss.'

'I don't even know why I told you all that,' she said, shaking her head. 'I don't know what I was thinking, but I do know this. I do not want you to do that again!'

'Holly, I—'

'I don't want your pity. And I do not want your kisses!'

'Holly!'

'It's time we went home.'

She headed for the shore as quickly as she could, allowing for the safest placement of her feet and the least risk, and she knew she probably looked ridiculous sidestepping and dancing down the jetty, while all the time her heart thudded in her chest and her stomach flipped and flopped with every creak and groan of the timbers.

She hated jetties with a vengeance. Hated the movement and the creaking and the ever-present risk of being plunged into the sea at any moment.

But she hated men who thought she was part of the package deal even more.

Ten years. Ten years since Gus had turned down Mark Turner's offer and he'd walked out of her life with not even a goodbye and still the only man she could find who was interested in kissing her was far more interested in the vines and the wines.

Nothing had changed in ten long years.

God!

Franco had kissed her.

Why? He didn't even like her. She sure as hell didn't like him.

Especially now.

'Holly,' he said alongside her, because of course she was never going to outrun his irritatingly long legs. 'What is your problem? It's not such a big deal.'

Maybe not to him.

'Holly, it meant nothing.'

No, it never did apparently.

'Holly!' He hooked his fingers around one elbow and swung her around to face him. 'What's wrong?'

'I'm not stupid, you know.'

'I know that.'

'I'm not part of this deal and you better remember that.'

'I never thought you were.'

'And I certainly won't be signing that contract any sooner just because you think I'm so naive I might be flattered that a Chatsfield pays me a little attention.'

'I do not think that!'

'Good. Keep on not thinking that and there's a chance we might even survive this six weeks of hell you're putting us through. Now, let me go and get out of my way.'

'With pleasure,' he snarled, dropping her arm and stepping clear and watching her pick her way as quickly as she could down the jetty.

Why had he kissed her? He asked himself the same question, examined it from every angle and from back to front, and still he could come up with no logical explanation. A mere impulse didn't cut it. He'd heard sad stories before and not been moved to kiss the person telling them, so why today? Why with this woman, someone who already had reason to hate him? And while he didn't care what she thought of him personally, why would he risk getting her back up? What the hell was wrong with him?

An impulse. A stupid impulse. But it didn't make him any happier knowing that this time he couldn't blame it on jet lag.

She stumbled her way along the timbers, hating jetties and creaking timbers and men who only wanted to take advantage. But the thing that she hated most of all was a man who tasted so good that she hadn't wanted to stop.

Where had that come from?

He was a Chatsfield, for heaven's sake!

The worst kind of man.

And he had some kind of nerve to think she was going to fall at his feet.

They barely spoke on the way back, an hour of excruciating tension, where thoughts seemed louder than words and where every breath reminded her of how good this man had tasted.

God, but she was a fool. She'd watched his face descend. She'd known without a shadow of a doubt he was going to kiss her, and like a rabbit stuck in headlights, she'd stood there transfixed, waiting for it to happen.

Willing it to happen.

What the hell was wrong with her?

Finally came the turn-off for the driveway into Purman Wines and then the house came into sight, and never had she been happier to escape from a car. Never had she been happier to escape from any man and her own stupidity. She slammed the heavy door behind her and crunched up the gravel driveway when she heard another door bang shut, and she was about to swing around and tell Franco he could take the car to the cottage and save walking if he wanted—either way, she just wanted him gone—when the door swung open and a ruddy-faced Gus called out, 'Holly, there you are. Hurry up, there's a phone call for you!'

'Who is it?' she called, more concerned about whether Franco was taking her advice and making himself scarce than whoever was on the phone.

'Hurry!'

Whatever it was, he was bursting with it.

'Franco, don't go. Not yet. I think you'll want to hear this too.'

Hear what? thought Holly as Gus handed her the receiver. 'Holly Purman speaking.'

Holly listened. Made an appropriate noise every now and then to show she was still paying attention, but given the way her blood was whooshing past her ears, really she'd stopped taking anything in after the first sentence.

'Thank you,' she said at last, severing the call as Gus beamed at her and Franco stood behind, looked bemused.

'Well?' asked Gus, who looked fit to burst.

'That was Russell Armitage from the Australian Wine Federation,' she said, feeling more than a little dazed.

'And?'

She looked at Pop, the man who had raised her since she was a toddler, the man who had taught her everything she knew, and she knew this was as much for him as it was for her.

She let go a smile so wide it brought tears to her eyes. 'And I've just been nominated for winemaker of the year!' She jumped into the air squealing, fists punching the air, before she threw herself down alongside his wheelchair and planted her arms around her grandfather's neck.

'I knew it!' Gus said, laughing, clapping her on the back. 'I knew it when he rang but he wouldn't tell me why, he insisted on talking to you. I was so glad when I heard the car. Oh, Holly, I'm so proud of you! You should have been nominated last year. I always said you were robbed. This is your year!'

She sniffed and rubbed cheeks damp from tears of joy as she rose. 'This is only a nomination, Pop. There are six nominees, remember. I'm up against some pretty stiff competition.'

'But you deserve it the most, my girl,' he said. 'But what am I thinking? This calls for a celebration!' Gus wheeled off to the fridge in search of a bottle of bubbles, leaving her standing, still wiping tears from her face.

'Well done,' Franco said stiffly, holding out his hand to shake hers. 'That's quite an achievement.'

Gus growled from over at the fridge. 'That's hardly a way to congratulate someone who's just been nominated for winemaker of the year. Can't you do better than that, Franco?'

And he would have shaken his head and excused himself, so fresh were his memories of that kiss at the jetty, and so raw his psyche after scratching away at it for an explanation, that he just wanted to remove himself and let it crust over and heal—he would have, except that instead of hostility in her eyes, he saw them flare with something like panic, something that told him all was not what it seemed.

He forced a smile then, curious as to what she might be so scared of. Besides, he was never one to turn away from a challenge. 'Of course I can.'

Turquoise eyes widened. Pink lips pursed.

'Congratulations, Holly,' he said. She was like a board when he pulled her against him, as tight and stiff as some of the timbers on the jetty where they'd walked this day. But like other timbers, there was give in her too. He could feel it now as he pressed his lips chastely to her cheek, feel the give in her resolve, the wavering, the weakness under the rigid cladding while the tide swirled and eddied below.

Just as he could feel the firm breasts under that drab polo jumper brush against his chest, the promise of wonders, and he knew there was a lot more to this woman than met the eye.

Oh, yes, Holly Purman was all kinds of surprise package.

He released her then, and Gus laughed. 'That's more like it.'

Holly didn't think so.

Holly didn't think so one little bit.

She busied herself collecting glasses, feeling her cheeks burn and her breasts tingle and the rush of being announced a finalist swamped by a rush of an entirely different sort. And she realised that the reaction she'd had to his oh-so-brief kiss on the end of a windswept jetty hadn't been an aberration.

Damn.

'So how long before the winner is announced?' Gus asked as he popped the cork.

Holly dragged her mind back over the blurred conversation. 'Three weeks, I think he mentioned. He apologised because it was such short notice this year but one of the judges was overseas.'

'And the announcement will be made in Sydney as usual?'

'The Opera House. They'll fly us over.'

Gus frowned as he poured the straw-coloured wine into the three flutes. 'I hope I'll be fit enough to travel.'

'Of course you will, Pop. You have to be there for the big announcement.'

'Then I guess I'd just better be there, hadn't I.' He raised his glass to his granddaughter. 'To Holly Purman, wine whisperer, Dionysus's handmaiden and soon-to-be Australian Winemaker of the Year!'

'Pop,' she warned, holding up one hand, but he shooshed her with another toast, louder this time, laden with pride.

'To Holly Purman, Angus Purman's brilliant granddaughter!'

'To Holly,' said Franco, and Holly buzzed on so many different levels. She'd been nominated for the industry's highest accolade, not just an acknowledgement of everything she and Pop had worked towards, but a recognition by her industry peers of her talent as a winemaker. And she buzzed because of the pride she saw in her grandfather's smiling face—she knew she'd made up for the grief she'd given him over the years, just like she'd promised to do.

And then, over the flute of sparkling wine she was tipping against her bottom lip, grey eyes met hers—grey eyes that said her secret rush had been no secret and that he knew—and she buzzed anew.

It was harder working in the days that followed. It was impossible to ignore him. It was impossible to forget about him. It was impossible not to look and follow his progress whenever he moved past her field of vision. Impossible not to be caught watching and to look away too late.

Quite simply she was fascinated by everything about him, by the way he moved in those moleskin jeans, by the way he held on to a pair of snips with those long-fingered hands, and by that velvet voice with its continental notes. He was a Chatsfield and yet he wasn't, at least not the way she'd expected a Chatsfield to be. He worked as hard in the vineyard as anybody she knew. He lived quietly in the cottage or went into town with Josh in the evenings from what she could tell.

And he curled her stomach into knots every time she caught him looking at her or when their hands brushed while reaching for the snips.

And it was a kind of hell.

One week down, Franco figured as he sipped on a mug of steaming coffee during break, which left five or there-abouts to go, and the pruning would be done and he'd have that contract signed and be on his way home.

Once upon a time he would have said he could hardly wait but he was enjoying working in a vineyard again after being part of management for so long, especially in such a different part of the world, and five weeks would soon pass quickly enough.

Besides, the job had just got more interesting. Holly Purman was the prickliest woman he'd met—on the outside. On the inside? Well, she'd told him she didn't want him to kiss her but he'd felt something there. She'd told him she didn't like him but those turquoise eyes that followed him around the vineyard weren't exactly sending a hail of razor blades his way. Not any more.

But as to how much more interesting it would get? Who

could say, but maybe those five weeks wouldn't be a complete waste of time.

'More coffee?' offered Josh, and Franco nodded. The hot brew sent curls of steam rising into the damp air. 'So Holly left you out here on your own?'

'Just while she handles another of those radio interviews.' There'd been at least a dozen of them since the announcement of the finalists. 'She'll be here any minute.'

'Still,' the other man said, pouring himself a mug and helping himself to a piece of fruitcake, 'that's quite something. Holly doesn't trust just anybody with her vines.'

'I had noticed.'

'She must think you're pretty damned good.'

Were they talking about the same Holly Purman? Who knew how her mind worked? Not him. 'I'm not so sure about that.'

The pair drank their coffee in silence for a while before Josh said, 'Did you hear about the party?'

'What party?'

'Mamma Angela, Angela Ciavaro, from next door is throwing a party for Holly Friday night, to celebrate her nomination. Everyone in the district is invited.'

'Well, if everyone's invited, I guess that means I'll be there too.'

Josh just nodded, munching on his cake, sipping on his coffee. 'You like her, don't you?'

Where the hell was this going? Was Josh still fretting about that stupid hair tie? 'Who, Angela?' he said, being deliberately obtuse. 'I've never met her.'

'No. Holly. You like Holly.'

And if Franco had ever had a twitch in his eye, it would have been twitching like mad now. 'She's all right,' he said, choosing his words ultracarefully. 'She and Gus clearly make a great team—with your help, of course.'

'Only we all like her around here.'

He nodded. 'Ri-ight.' And swirled the coffee in his cup and drank some more.

'But she got burned once. By this rich guy who promised her the world. Only what he really wanted was the vines.'

Somewhere in a gum tree nearby a kookaburra laughed and Franco found himself half wondering whether that was entirely coincidental.

He guessed enough to know whatever had happened back then hadn't ended well. And now he was being warned.

'I have no intention of hurting Holly, if that's what you're worried about.'

The other man stood, looked abashed, not expecting a direct answer to his indirect line of enquiry. 'Good. Well, I better be getting back.'

Franco just swallowed the dregs of his coffee, bitter and cold, with the chorus of the kookaburra playing in his head.

CHAPTER EIGHT

THE FORECAST WAS for wall-to-wall rain, a huge low stuck over the southeast region of the state, and Holly decided they'd be better off getting the sparkling wine order for the Port MacDonnell wedding settled and come back to the pruning when there was a break in the weather.

They left at six in the morning, the rain already pelting down, the wipers going overtime. With a good run they should be at Purman's Adelaide Hills vineyard by lunchtime.

Except there was a truck rollover on the highway and the backtracking and the diversion cost them another two hours, so it was mid-afternoon by the time Franco took the Crafers exit from the South Eastern Freeway and followed Holly's directions through the picturesque Adelaide Hills towns of Piccadilly and Summertown.

Travel weary, Holly was wondering how they were going to make it back the same day. It was always going to be a long day without the delays and now they faced the prospect of not getting home before midnight, hard going on the rain-slick roads.

The sensible thing to do would be to stay overnight and drive back tomorrow fresh. The key to the guest suite they'd built for just such overnight stops was on the car keys. Then she glanced at the man alongside her, at his long-fingered hands on the wheel, at his strong too-perfect profile, and felt that strange clenching inside and looked away.

Then again, maybe that wouldn't be quite so sensible, and if Holly Purman could be summed up in just one word, *sensible* was probably the one. Maybe it was because she didn't have brothers or sisters or maybe it was because she'd grown up with Pop and was used to adult company, but she'd been that way as long as she could remember.

And staying overnight would definitely not be sensible.

She stole another glance at him and gazed at his lips and thought about the feel of his kiss and felt a shivery tingle blossom inside her. Then again, sensible had never felt like this.

Maybe sensible was overrated.

And maybe it was time to throw caution to the wind.

She sucked down air and gazed out her window, her cheeks burning, wondering if it was a kind of madness to be thinking what she was thinking. To be contemplating sleeping with a man she'd once considered her enemy.

It must be some kind of madness. But then it made a kind of sense too. He was no longer the enemy. He was... Franco—the man who worked the vines with her, the man who stirred her slumbering femininity as nobody ever had.

But best of all, he'd be gone soon, and nobody need ever know.

But would he even want to?

'This is more like the kind of country I'm used to,' Franco said alongside her, interrupting her thoughts. The land here dipped and rose, valley floors planted as market gardens, hillsides under orchard or vines, interspersed with pockets of bush. 'Without the benefit of your gum trees.'

Holly's ears pricked up. Beyond offering a name of the region, Franco had never willingly spoken of where he lived. Previously he'd clamped if the conversation edged anywhere near his life back in Italy or his family for that matter. It had irritated her at the time but she hadn't been interested enough to persist. He'd been something to be tolerated for the duration, that was all. But that was before, when she'd thought of him more as an inconvenience than a man. Now the man seemed front and centre of her imagination. Now she wanted to know all she could about him.

'It must be beautiful where you come from.'

'You've never been to Italy?'

She shook her head. 'I've never been overseas.'

'Never?'

She shook her head again. 'There was never the money. And then, when things improved, there was never the time.' She indicated he should turn right at the next intersection and then asked, 'Is it the Piacenza region where your mother comes from as well?'

He slowed, waiting for an oncoming car to pass before he could make the turn. 'Why do you ask that?'

'Well, your mother is Italian and you're living in Italy and I thought—well, I just wondered...'

'She came from that region, yes.'

'She's not there now?'

'Not as far as I can tell.'

'You...don't know where she is?'

'Nobody knows where she is.'

Holly blinked. 'But surely...?'

He cursed in Italian under his breath, a curse he'd heard his mother fling at his father when he was just a child, before he answered, his mood as wintry as the thick atmosphere and the heavy sky. 'Nobody knows,' he snapped. 'Now, which way at this next intersection?'

She sank back into her seat. 'Straight ahead, then right at the next town.'

She shut up then, thank God, giving him the breathing space to get his temperature under control. As if eight hours stuck alongside her in the car wasn't enough, now she had to bring up his mother, scratching away at wounds that were best left alone.

Who knew where his mother was? Who knew if she was alive or dead? Not him. Sure, he might have wondered once, might have imagined or even hoped as a rebellious teenager that he'd find her hiding out amongst the hills and vineyards of Piacenza, but that was a long time ago and he'd long ceased wondering.

After all, why should he care after the woman had walked out on the family and left them all to rot?

Was it any wonder his siblings had gone wild? Rich, good-looking, untamed. Was it any wonder they could fill gossip magazines all by themselves?

He snorted. Not that he'd been much better.

The apple doesn't fall far from the tree.

Whoever had coined that phrase knew what they were talking about. But thank God he'd managed to keep his private life private. Thank God the paparazzi had long given up on him as the boring Chatsfield by the time Michele had turned up on his doorstep needing help.

He felt a familiar ache in his side, not helped by sitting so long in the car. He didn't want to think about Michele. He didn't want to think about that year. That loss.

The woman beside him shifted in her seat and he caught a whiff of her scent, something light and lemony and fresh. Like she was, he thought. Natural and unspoilt and so different to the type of women he was usually attracted to.

He hadn't set out to be attracted to her, and yet...

He turned his head. She was staring straight ahead, her arms crossed, and if he didn't know better he'd think she was sulking.

Maybe he'd been a bit hard on her, but after eight hours sitting so close it was no wonder he was feeling on edge.

He changed down a gear for a bend and let his fingers stray, his fingertips just grazing the fabric of her work pants. She jumped like he'd branded her and he smiled.

Josh had tried to warn him off and he'd listened. He hadn't set out to seduce anyone, let alone prickly Ms Purman, and he didn't resent getting the warning. But then he remembered that stolen kiss and he'd seen the way she'd watched him all this week. He'd seen the desire and the longing building in their blue depths while he'd been thinking about her in ways that weren't entirely honourable himself. Did she realise those eyes were like windows to her thoughts?

And Josh had mentioned nothing about consenting adults.

Not that she was likely to consent to anything right now, and with good reason. 'I'm sorry, I don't talk much about my mother. I generally don't talk about my family at all.'

'I noticed,' she said, her head swinging around. 'Why is that?'

He shrugged, slowing the car as they came up behind a fruit-and-vegetable truck that was struggling along the windy road. 'I don't have a lot to do with them. Any of them.'

'Why not? Because you don't approve of their lifestyle?'

He had never approved, he'd always thought he was better than that—until Michele had appeared out of the blue—but that wasn't the reason. 'I left home when I was sixteen. I was angry and rebellious and decided I didn't want to live in a media circus any more.'

She sighed and sat back in her seat. 'If I had brothers and sisters I'd see them all the time. I'd love to be part of a big family.'

'What? Even if it was a family like the Chatsfields?'

'They'd still be my family. I can imagine Christmas with a house fit to bursting and everybody talking at once and lashings of food on the table. You're so lucky.'

Was he? He'd never felt lucky. He'd felt…lost—like he'd never belonged. So he'd turned his back on being one of a crowd and fought hard to forge his own identity, fighting to get himself and keep himself out of the limelight.

But now he wondered about his family. He knew what the magazines said about them, but how were they really? Antonio, Lucilla and Nicolo—he didn't even know if they had partners or were married. And what of his younger siblings, the twins, Orsino and Lucca, and Cara, who had been only seven when he had left?

Only one year older than Nikki when she had died.

He swallowed. Did Cara even remember him? Remember the games of cricket they'd played before he'd left? Remember the warnings he'd tried to give her about the big bad world around them?

And then Holly said something that sounded like *koala* but she was so casual he thought he must have misheard until she pointed and he was glad the truck in front was going too slowly because he saw it curled high up in a tree.

She spotted another a little farther along, this time with a baby clutched to its mother's chest.

Nikki would have been beside herself. She'd loved animals, large and small, and he and Michele had taken her to the zoo as many times as her failing body would allow. When she'd seen her first real live koala, she'd grinned so hard her little face had nearly split in two.

He found a place to pull off and they walked back for a closer look. The mother koala chewed on a gum leaf and blinked at them unconcerned while the joey slept oblivious on her chest. He took a photo for Nikki, even though his daughter would never see it, but the other children in Nikki's Ward would no doubt enjoy it.

'A souvenir of your trip?' she asked.

'Something for a friend,' he said, and left it at that.

They walked back to the car and he listened as Holly told him about the koalas, her delight in the furry creatures palpable, and it shook off his melancholy. He liked the way she looked when she was happy. He liked what it did to light up her turquoise eyes and put colour in those sensual lips.

He wondered what it would be like to be the one to make her eyes light up like that and put a flush in those pink cheeks. And he wondered whether he might soon get to find out.

'A couple more kilometres down this road,' she said back in the car and after they'd made the final turn. 'You'll see our sign out front.'

They drove along a winding valley lined by towering eucalyptus trees with creamy smooth trunks, stately and majestic.

'Candlebark gums,' she told him when he mentioned them in passing. 'Eucalyptus rubida.'

He recognised it. 'The name of your sparkling wine.'

'Ten out of ten,' she said with a smile, sounding impressed. 'We wanted a name that reflected this area. And the vines sit shoulder to shoulder with the candlebarks—it just seemed a natural fit.'

He turned up the long driveway, towards a house set up high on one side beyond which vines marched up the hillside.

'The manager's away on holiday with his family right now so you can park anywhere.'

'We've got the whole place to ourselves?'

It was a test. He'd intended it to be one. It would either mean nothing to her, or something.

She blinked, a delicious blush colouring her cheeks, the tip of her pink tongue hovering tremulously at her top lip.

Bullseye.

She cleared her throat. Avoided his eyes. 'It actually means we should be able to get this wine disgorged and dosaged without interruption and be back on the road in no time.'

It was a reasonable answer, she thought, under the circumstances. It was the right answer if you were thinking about the job at hand and not about the humming in your veins and vague possibilities that he might not even have intended.

And if he had meant anything else, she'd soon know it.

'After the delays on the highway, you think we'll get everything done and make it back today?'

His eyes had a glint to them, his lips a faint curve, and his words put her in mind of another answer and reminded her of the key to the guesthouse weighing heavily on her conscience.

Because between the heavy sky and sodden earth, between the barren vines and the towering gums, something had changed between them. There was an added note to his voice, mischievous. Challenging. Maybe even daring.

Making him seem more playful than ever.

Infinitely more interesting.

And infinitely more dangerous.

Did she dare test it?

She'd never been so tempted.

But what kind of fool would she look if she gave in to temptation. What was in it for her? Making love to this man—a Chatsfield of all people—after all she'd said about the family? Wasn't that some kind of surrender after he'd blown into their lives, practically demanding the keys to the estate, and she'd done everything she possibly could to fight him off?

How would it look if she slept with the man now?

And yet still she felt the pull and the lure of him, with every fibre of her being.

'Let's see how far we get,' she said, not even wanting to think how that could be construed as she jumped from the car.

The air was cold and sharp, her breath turning to mist. They only needed ten dozen bottles and a couple extra for the cellar door supply. It shouldn't take long with Franco to help her.

And they could be back on the road again tonight, or they wouldn't...

She took the path around the house and headed straight to the stone building behind, and if the outside of it reminded him of an old French barn, the inside was some kind of sparkling wine lover's paradise. She snapped on lights and the bottle neck freezer and went to fiddle with a fireplace and get some heat into the place while he was content to turn in a circle and breathe it all in.

Slate floor, exposed timber beams and riddling racks lining the stone walls, the racks set on a gentle slope with bottles standing upside down inside them on an angle. Hundreds and hundreds of bottles. Instinctively his hand reached out for one bottle, giving it the slightest of shakes and a quarter turn.

Apparently she noticed. 'You can give me a hand with the riddling while we're waiting for the freezer to get cold enough for the disgorging,' she said as the fire in the stove caught, sending an orange glow into the room and illuminating artworks hanging above the racks.

'This is something,' he said, honestly impressed. 'I knew you had a vineyard up here, but this?'

'You like it? I don't get to spend a whole lot of time here, but this baby is my pride and joy. Gus wasn't keen being so far from our Coonawarra operation, but a decent sparkling was the one thing we didn't have in our arsenal.'

'What does he think now?'

She lifted an eyebrow. 'Seriously?'

He smiled back. She was right, stupid question. The longer he was here, the more he was impressed with what this woman had achieved with her vines and her wines. He could scarcely believe he'd ever thought of her as drab. Maybe because that was before he'd stumbled upon the colour in her turquoise eyes and her pink lips. Maybe because, when she smiled, she looked anything but drab.

He forced his attention back to the bottles lining the wall. 'When was this lot bottled?'

He watched her lightly run her hand over a row of bottles as she walked along, almost as if she was caressing them. The wine whisperer at work. But that wasn't the only thing he noticed. Because there was a sway in those hips as she moved. Subtle but there. And he knew that somewhere under those khaki clothes hid the body of a woman, curvy and lush.

She was mad if she thought they were going anywhere tonight.

'If you're talking this year's vintage, not that long ago. After we picked, the juice spent five months in new French oak barrels before being bottled. So they're still young and we'll just leave them on lees. The longer on lees, the more biscuity the wine, so there's no rush.' And then she stopped and smiled. 'But you know all that already.'

He did, but he liked listening to her nonetheless. He'd met plenty of winemakers in his time, some of them pompous old toads who liked to think themselves geniuses. But Holly made what she did sound simple, as if anyone could do it. He knew differently. There was a science to wine-making, of course, but there was also an art. A magic.

Holly had that magic, in spades.

And he itched to hold that magic in his hands and feel it when she came apart. Was there a chance it might happen tonight?

With a wrench he forced his mind back to the wine.

'You do all your disgorging here?' It seemed hard to believe they could run such a successful operation from two such modest sites.

'Mostly. It works fine. Unless someone makes a big order, we usually only dosage a few dozen at a time. We'll fill this order from last year's vintage and I reckon it'll go down a treat at that wedding.'

'How do you propose filling the Chatsfield order the way you now work?'

The lights in her eyes flared. 'You mean, how do I propose filling the order if I sign the contract?'

Once upon a time, not so long ago, that argument would have been a whole lot more convincing.

'Do you really think there's any doubt now?'

She turned away, her hand sweeping over bottle bases like they were her children. 'We'll disgorge and dosage in bigger lots, that's all. Freight over several dozen at a time. But still, the plan will be to keep the wine on lees as long as possible. I'm not into factory-scale production. That's not the way we operate, and I'm guessing it's not the reason why Chatsfield Hotels picked us as their chosen supplier.'

She turned around a beat later, her eyes showing that she'd met his challenge head-on and faced it down. Her turquoise eyes gleamed in the light of the fire. 'And now we'd better get this show on the road.'

Holly took one side of the room, Franco the other. They worked quickly without rushing, turning bottles a quarter turn to shift the lees in the neck of the bottle so it didn't get stuck in the microscopic ridges in the glass, and with the pot-bellied stove crackling away and pumping out heat, soon it didn't feel cold in the room at all.

They made a pretty good team, she thought, aware of the fluid movements of the man on the other side of the room moving to the rhythmic sounds of glass bumping against wood.

He'd stripped off his jacket and his shirt hugged his broad shoulders as he reached up to the highest bottles, the fabric pulling tight down his back to the belted mole-skins he looked so good in.

If he made a move on her tonight, would she take it?

Should she?

He glanced over his shoulder and caught her spying on him. He smiled. 'Checking up on me?'

She smiled back. 'Yes.'

He laughed and turned back around, and she smiled at the bottles on the wall and had to remember to breathe.

What was she thinking?

He was a Chatsfield.

And yes, he was that, but he was also as good-looking as sin and he'd be gone in a few short weeks and it wasn't like she really had to like him.

And when it all came down to it, she didn't really dislike him. Not any more. Otherwise she couldn't even begin to consider the germ of the idea that had been spinning in her mind all day. Sure, she hated the way he'd turned up, expecting them all to fall at his feet and hand over all that he'd expected, but he was more than that. He'd proven it in the couple of weeks since with a work ethic she never would have believed possible.

As for what was in it for her, well, if he was interested, it might even help her out with something that had been worrying her for a while.

He seemed interested...

And then they ran out of bottles and she checked the temperature in the freezer and declared it cold enough to freeze the neck of the bottles and they started the real work, placing bottles neck-down into the freezing liquid.

She'd planned the workspace to suit herself. There was no automated production line like you'd find in a factory set up for big volume processing. This was a boutique enterprise and the boutique label meant that the disgorging, dosaging, corking and caging functions were all wedged between the freezer and a bar topped by a single massive slab of timber.

Working by herself had never presented any problems.

Working with Franco was a different matter.

He seemed to be everywhere in the small space, his long arms never far away or his big feet taking up the floor, and there was no way that two bodies sharing the task wouldn't brush, contact or otherwise collide with each other along the way.

For a woman hovering on the cusp of one of the most important decisions in her life, it was proof positive that she hadn't lost her ability to make a decision based on sound, sensible criteria. Not when a brush of fabric against fabric, or skin against skin, sent her senses humming and her skin tingling all the way to her bones. Not when the touches seemed not always to be accidental—and they were the most shimmying, tingly contacts of all, when she would look up and see him watching her and feel the heat all the way down to her toes.

Somehow some part of her stayed focused enough to concentrate on the job. Somehow they managed to establish a routine. He passed her the bottle from the freezer, the lees trapped in the frozen neck of the bottle, and she flipped the crown seal releasing the frozen plug of lees into the keg-shaped disgorging booth, before dosaging the wine with the sweet liqueur. After which Franco corked it and twisted on the muselet, the metal cage that held down the cork under pressure. They had to work quickly. The tricky bit was not letting the pressurised contents shoot out after the crown seal blew off or after the wine had been dosaged, but Holly was a pro at this job and she didn't lose a drop.

They worked through the order, an ever-growing stash of cartons building up, cartons filled with bottles that could wait until they got home to label.

They worked and brushed and touched and got in each other's way and exchanged heated glances and somehow made it through the order and another dozen until there was only one more box to be done.

'Last dozen,' he said, pulling the first of the dozen from the neck freezer and wiping it free of the solution before handing it to her.

She took it from him and grabbed her bottle top remover, snapping off the lid and the frozen lees into the disgorging bin and covering the opening with her thumb before she dosaged. 'We'll be done in no time at this rate.'

'We make a good team.'

A moment's hesitation before she handed back the bottle for corking. His fingers brushed hers as he took the bottle and she tingled. 'You're not bad at this,' she said, feeling flushed with success at getting through the job so quickly, feeling emboldened by the clandestine and not so clandestine touches along the way. 'For a Chatsfield, I mean.'

'You're not so bad yourself,' he said, bottle positioned ready to be corked.

'You mean, I'm not bad for an intransigent, uncooperative, stubborn woman?'

He hesitated, his hand poised ready to press the lever.
'Did I really say that?'

'You really did.'

He had the nerve to smile and the heat under her skin
had nothing to do with the fire in the pot-bellied stove as it
burned all the way to her toes. 'What the hell was I thinking?' He pushed down on the press and the cork pushed
into the tight neck of the bottle and stuck fast. She sucked
in air, trying her hardest not to make a sound.

And she knew she'd never cork another bottle without
thinking of this man and sex.

She watched, her cheeks on fire, as he twisted the muselet tight with the applicator as expertly as she would have.

God, but he had gorgeous hands. Talented, long-fingered hands. If she played her cards right, those long-fingered hands could soon be on her.

She sucked in air in a whoosh.

How could she play her cards right when she didn't
know how this game worked? Seduction was a stranger to
her, foreign and unknown and not to be trusted.

He swung around to pass her another bottle and brushed
against her shirt and her breasts tightened and tingled and
told her that seduction would take care of itself.

Thank God for instinct, she thought as she took it, disgorged and dosaged, grateful to have something real to
concentrate on as she passed it back. Something concrete.

Ten more bottles, counting down.

They didn't talk. There was no need. The not so accidental brushes of skin and cloth did the talking. And with
every bottle the tension built until the air fairly crackled
around them.

And then there was one.

CHAPTER NINE

FRANCO PASSED THE bottle to her reverently, his grey eyes the colour of the clouds that had scudded across the same storm-tossed sky the day he'd arrived, ripe with intent, ready to unleash their load.

She swallowed, her throat suddenly tight and dry, took the bottle from his hands and could feel those eyes on her back, through the layers of her clothes, warm upon her skin. The bottle opener slipped from her shaking hands and clattered to the floor

He picked it up, coming up so close that she couldn't breathe, his eyes not leaving hers. 'You dropped something,' he murmured, so close to her face that she could feel his warm breath on her cheek. Her tongue flicked out to see if he tasted as good as she remembered.

He didn't taste as good.

He tasted better.

'Thank you,' she whispered as their hands connected around the shaft of the opener, their eyes connected on another level. Vaguely she was aware they hadn't finished, that there was one bottle in her hand left to disgorge, a bottle opener poised.

Just one more bottle.

It would only take a second.

But the hand curling around her neck, the fingers sliding through her hair, demanded her attention. His lips demanded her focus.

And if she could just get this bottle out of the way, then her hands would be free, like his. Right now she wished her hands were free to slide around his neck and up his chest.

Then his fingers in her hair drew her towards him and his lips came closer, and dammit, she needed her hands to be free.

It would only take a second.

The bottle cap and the lees shot into the booth. She covered the top with her thumb. Swung the bottle—she really could do this in her sleep—and dosaged the bottle the very same second his mouth met hers and she sighed into his kiss, and of the two incidents, the kiss was the more compelling, his lips opening, inviting hers to follow his lead, and she was all too willing to follow. Until wine under pressure sprayed from the bottle and by the time Holly remembered she should have covered the top, they were showered with the freshly dosaged wine. And they were both shocked and sticky and laughing as he took the fizzing bottle from her hand and parked it safely away on the bench where it could do no more harm.

Her heart was thudding a million miles an hour, blood fizzing and under pressure in her veins like the wine in the bottle when he stopped laughing and put his hands to his lips and tasted and frowned. 'It needs something,' he said before he took her face in his hands and sampled her lips, his tongue sweeping their width. 'Perfect,' he declared, and pulled her hard against him.

She went willingly. He tasted of the wine and of the liqueur they used to replace the sweetness; he tasted of warm skin and hot breath, and of grape juice, fermented and strong, on his hot lips and his even hotter mouth.

She tasted pressure, hot and hard, and she liked it.

She felt herself pushed up against the bench top and she revelled in it, his chest hard against hers, knowing there was nowhere else to go, nowhere to run, even if she had half a mind to.

She wasn't running anywhere.

Not while he made her feel this way, tossed and tumbled on a sea of sensation, while his hands were in her hair, on her shoulders and her back and pressing him to her. Pressing her so close she could feel his hot hard length at her belly while his tongue worked magic in her mouth.

It was as shocking as it was compelling and she whimpered into his mouth, grinding her hips against him in spite of a fear borne of the ages, a fear of the unknown, while her actions were purely driven by need, needing to be closer, ever closer, and he obliged by grabbing her behind in his hands as his mouth plundered hers.

And then he used those hands to lift her and sit her on top of the timber slab and pull her legs around him.

His face was level with her breasts, and he cupped their fullness, and all he wanted to do was bury his head in those breasts, without the layers overladen.

'You're all wet and sticky,' he said. 'We should get you out of these wet clothes.'

He could rip them off now, he thought. He ached to discover the woman he'd suspected had been lurking below all the time, but travelling in a car tomorrow with a woman in shredded clothes or returning her to her grandfather that way was so not a good look.

He put his hands to the hem of her polo top instead, resigned to going the slow way.

He peeled it from her, his lips never leaving hers until the last possible moment when he reefed it over her head.

And then he gazed, his eyes wide open.

He hadn't really thought about it, but if he had, he would

have imagined her underwear to be as dreary as her outerwear. Serviceable. Probably coloured in beige or khaki. No doubt with a Purman Wine logo emblazoned somewhere thereon.

If he had thought along those lines, he would have been wrong.

Very wrong.

Because instead of dreary, his eyes feasted on the extraordinary.

It wasn't really a bra. Not in the strict engineering sense of the word. Rather it was more of a confection—of creamy satin and black floral lace woven with a pink ribbon and tied in the middle in a little pink bow—and all cradling creamy smooth-skinned mounds of flesh beneath.

'Oh. My. God,' he said.

'Do you like it?' she asked, her teeth chewing her lip.

He glanced up at her with disbelief. 'I love it,' he growled, skimming his hands up the curves of her bare sides until his thumbs grazed the undersides of her breasts. Breath hissed through her teeth and he looked up to her face and saw what looked like ecstasy mixed with fear, but why should she look tense? How could she possibly imagine he wouldn't like what he saw?

His hands cupped her breasts and she shuddered. He pulled her closer, and pressed his lips to the skin of each mound and she gasped and then he pulled her head down and sucked her into his kiss.

'Please tell me you're wearing matching underwear,' he said when he could bear to tear his mouth away.

'I always wear matching underwear.'

His hardness twitched. God, and he'd never once suspected.

She was all kinds of surprise package. What other surprises was little Ms Holly Purman hiding?

He could hardly wait to find out.

Though this was hardly the place.

They were both sticky with wine and the timber bench was cold and there wasn't so much as a sofa, and while the fire was warming it was lacking the obligatory rug of seduction and it wasn't what he wanted right now.

Because he could do her on that bench top—and, oh, God, how he wanted to do her on that bench top right now—but it would get uncomfortable very fast.

He didn't want it getting uncomfortable any time soon.

He wanted somewhere entirely more comfortable.

'Is there a bed anywhere in this place?' he murmured between kisses, his hands riding up her thighs, thumbs aiming straight for paradise.

'There's a guest suite,' she said, her breath too choppy for one entire sentence, 'in the house.' Another breath. 'I've got a key.'

And the angels in his head sang a hallelujah chorus. He wrapped her sweater around her shoulders and collected her in his arms. 'Then what the hell are we doing here?'

The suite was perfect. Self-contained, spacious and, best of all, featuring a massive bed. It would do nicely.

But for now he bypassed the bed, kicking open the door to the en suite bathroom instead. Sticky had been fun for a while, but they'd moved beyond fun and now things were getting serious.

He put her gently down on her feet and snapped on the shower and water poured from a rainforest showerhead, the room soon fogging with steam.

Then he took her face in his hands and pressed his lips against hers and she trembled anew. His reaction to see-ing her in just her bra had warmed her from the inside out, an instant confidence booster, but she'd never been naked with a man before and she'd imagined they'd make love in a bed, covered up and with the lights out. But the lights were on and even the steam didn't hide a lot and the boost in her confidence was waning and she was once again apprehensive and afraid.

Was he intending to make love standing up in the shower?

And her oh-so-clever plan seemed more like a blundering mess.

She was so unskilled. So unpractised.

So uncertain as to what was expected of her. And it wasn't that she was worried so much about it being earth-shattering or even good the first time, because this wasn't so much about impressing Franco but more about getting the monkey off her back—the monkey that was riding shotgun on her shoulder now and that she wanted to be rid of—but still she didn't want to make a complete fool of herself in the process.

'You're trembling,' he said.

'I'm cold,' she lied.

He growled. 'I know how to warm you up.'

He did.

He sucked her into a kiss so deep she thought she'd drown, a kiss that made her forget for a moment that she was afraid, because he made her feel so good, he made this feel so right. Hands skimmed down her back, down to her waist and over her behind where his big hands lingered and then squeezed.

Dear God, she was drowning, but in sensation.

His hands were between them, at the buttons and fly of her trousers while his mouth worked some kind of magic on her neck, flicking tongue and hot mouth working in concert to lull her into thinking this would be easy—conspiring to make her forget how to think.

She didn't want to think. She wanted to feel.

He was all of everything and he was the master and right now she was his student. But he was hers too, hers to explore with hungry hands and seeking fingers. She tugged at his shirt, wanting it off, wanting to explore that perfect chest she'd seen that first night in the cottage. She fiddled with buttons until they were undone and he assisted by shrugging it off, and for just a moment she was happy, her hands filled with the feel of him, the sculpted chest and smooth olive skin, roughened with hair she curled her fingers in.

Until that wasn't enough and she wanted more.

The steam swirled around them, beckoning.

The heat built between them.

And Holly dared venture south, one hand tentatively exploring, testing to see if that hardness she'd felt pressed against her was as good as it felt.

Franco growled into her mouth and anticipation bloomed hot and heavy in her flesh.

Her fingers curled over the bulge of his hard length and she gave thanks that what she'd heard about big feet was true. She was already anticipating how that might feel inside her.

She could not wait to find out.

Boots were kicked off in a rush, two pairs of trousers slid to the floor and were kicked away and Holly used her toes to peel off her socks.

'Oh, my God, Holly,' he said, holding her at arm's length, his eyes searing her flesh all the way down and all the way up again.

She might have said the same thing if only she'd been able to unglue her tongue from the roof of her mouth. He could have been one of those statues you saw in the museums, an ancient god carved in stone. If not for the long scar on one side above his hip, he was perfection. And she might have asked but there was one other big difference between Franco and all those ancient statues that she could tell, even hidden under a band of black elastic.

And then even that was gone.

She swallowed, afraid to look, desperate to look.

He made it easy. He put his hand behind her head and pulled the tie from her hair, fluffing out the sticky strands in his hands. Her head leaned towards his hand. 'That's better,' he said. 'Much better. I like your hair down. It frames your eyes and your mouth.'

His hands were behind her then, the hooks of her bra flicked expertly undone. He put his hands to her shoulders and eased the straps down, peeling it away from her breasts.

He sucked in air and her nipples tightened to bullets, but as to which one came first, she couldn't possibly tell. Then with a sweep of his hands the scrap of matching fabric that was her panties was gone too.

'Magnificent,' he said, and Holly was glad she had decided that it should be tonight with this man, because this man, with his knowledge of the world, with his film-star good looks and sexy accent, would make her first time something special, something to remember on the long nights to come after he was gone.

He drew her into the steaming water and that was another revelation. He squirted bath gel in his hands and surprised her by using it on her, slippery fingers on slippery skin, and everywhere he touched was alive and wanting.

He squirted gel into her hands to use on him, and she relished the chance to explore his body this way, mapping him with her hands, finding the places that made him growl, discovering the places that made him grab her wrist and made her wait.

She loved discovering those places most of all.

'What's this?' she said, curious as her fingers traced the long ridge of scar tissue at his side.

'Nothing,' he said, his hand at her wrist, pulling it away.

She didn't have time to wonder. Because now that the gel had done its work and the wine was gone from their skin and the stickiness from their hair, he used his tongue and mouth on her clean skin. She gasped when he backed her against the shower wall and blistered a trail of kisses down her throat to her breasts. She sighed as she closed her eyes and gave herself up to pleasure. She had never known the simple pleasure of a man taking her nipple in his mouth, a hot tongue circling that tight bud. She had never known of the link between nipples and that aching place between her thighs. She had never imagined the erotic pleasure of a man's tongue at her belly or how her legs could seem so restless and wanting to part.

No, *needing* to part.

And then his head dipped even lower and her head hit the wall behind her.

Oh, God, surely not that.

Her senses were at fever pitch. Nobody—but nobody—had ever touched her there, and he was going to with his...

His fingers gently parted her and, 'Oh, God!'

His tongue flicked hot and hard against a tiny nub of flesh that seemed to hold an entire warehouse of nerve endings and it was as if he'd just provoked every one into life.

Oh, God.

And then he swiped her again and she wished she was lying down, because all the sensation in her body was centred there and there was nothing left to make sure her knees would work.

She planted her hands in his hair, her fingers tangling in his waves, clutching him as he played her, flicking and circling, circling and flicking, needing stability in a world not only teetering on its axis, but flashing in bright colours.

The water cascaded over them, steam enveloped them and the temperature built to fever pitch and she wished he would stop but she wanted more, and he gave her more, with his lips around that exquisitely tight bud of nerve endings, sucking, inviting, and she cursed that weapon of sinful seduction that was his mouth.

Cursed it and blessed it as the colours intensified and the world teetered some more, and she hovered on an exquisite edge of nowhere.

Until she felt his hand—there—and the press of a searching fingertip at her core, felt the push and slide of intrusion and the strange unworldliness of it, and the strange auto-clenching answer of her muscles.

He seemed to hesitate then, his mouth stilled on her most secret of places, but it was already too late, her muscles already constricting, the colours brightening and the world already spinning out of control and there was no stopping them.

The orgasm slammed into her and cracked her head back hard against the wall. She didn't feel a thing. All her feelings were centred on the series of tidal waves that burst from her core and slammed into every part of her, leaving her limp and dazed and her body humming. And she was glad Franco was there to hold her, or she might have otherwise slid to the floor in a sodden, strength-obliterated mess.

She sagged against him like a rag doll as he turned off the taps, still too dazed to speak, still buzzing with the discovery that such pleasure existed, exquisite and intense, and the wonderment that if he had done that with his mouth, how would it feel to have him inside her?

He wrapped her in fluffy towels and lifted her in his arms and carried her to the bed in the next room.

Soon she would find out.

He dropped her on the bed a little more unceremoniously than she would have preferred. And then he turned
and headed straight back to the bathroom.

Through the open door she could see him give himself
a quick rub-down with a towel before flinging it on the
floor, and pulling on his underwear. A cold fear gripped
her heart and woke her from her daze.

'What are you doing?'

He thrust his long legs into his moleskins. 'What's it
look like? I'm getting dressed.'

She sat up, still wrapped in towels. 'Why? What's wrong?'

'When were you going to tell me?' he said, pulling on
socks and boots. 'Or were you just hoping I wouldn't notice?'

She pulled the towels up tighter around her breasts,
fear pulling what was left of her warm glow to shreds.
'Notice what?'

'That you've never done this before.'

She blinked away at moisture suddenly welling in her
eyes. She knew she was inexperienced but she'd hoped it
wouldn't be quite so obvious. 'Was I that bad?'

He growled in frustration as he pulled his shirt over his
shoulders and did up the buttons. 'Why didn't you tell me
you were a virgin?'

'Why should I tell you?'

'My God, Holly—' he pulled on socks and boots
'—because you're twenty-eight years old. Nobody would
expect you were still a virgin. What happened with that
man anyway?'

'What man?'

'The rich one—the one who only wanted the vines or
something.'

'Who the hell told you about him?'

'Josh did. He was warning me not to hurt you.'

'Oh, my God.' She put her hands to her face, morti-
fied that not only the details of one of the most humiliat-
ing episodes of her life was being discussed between the
menfolk, but that men were being warned off. Great. No
wonder she was still a virgin.

'So I never for one moment imagined you're a virgin. I
mean, you're twenty-eight years old. Nobody's still a virgin at twenty-eight.'

She might be a virgin but she wasn't some kind of freak
like he made out. 'You know this for a fact, do you? Or is
it just that you Chatsfields have different priorities to the
rest of us mere mortals. At what age are you expected to
lose your virginity? Eighteen? Twenty? Or do the tabloids
prefer you lose it even earlier?'

'That's rubbish.'

'How old were you, Franco?'

He shook his head. 'My family has got nothing to do
with this.'

'Why? Your family permeates every part of this deal.
Your family is the reason I didn't want this deal in the first
place. How can I leave your family out of it?'

He tucked his shirt into his jeans and bundled up her
clothes from the bathroom floor that he tossed onto the
bed beside her.

'This is about you and me. Nobody else.'

'So if it's about you and me, and nobody else, then why
can't you make love to me?'

'Because you're a virgin, Holly.'

'So what?'

'Isn't that enough?'

'What?' That was no kind of answer at all. 'So if I
wasn't a virgin, you'd be making love to me right now?'

He grunted a response, neither acceptance or denial, as

he threaded his fingers through his still-damp hair, looking anywhere but at her. 'I should go pack those cartons on the truck.'

'Why?' she demanded. 'Why does me being a virgin make any difference? You wanted to make love to me. God, you practically did. Why is it now a problem? Are you afraid of virgins?'

'Stop being so melodramatic. I'm not afraid of anything. I just don't mess with them. Get dressed.'

He was serious! He was actually going to walk away. 'What do you want me to do? Beg?'

'I want you to put your clothes on. We're leaving.'

Dammit, he could not do this to her. Not now. She'd been so close. So damned close. Talk about slamming the door before the horse had bolted.

Holly leapt from the cover of her towels and for the first time in her life didn't care that she was bare or exposed or naked, because she was so angry. Besides, perhaps he needed a reminder of what he was missing out on.

Tremulously she stood naked in the centre of the room, her hands open by her sides.

'You wanted to make love to me,' she said, offering herself to him.

His eyes danced and flickered around the fringes of her. 'Sure. Right up until I found out about your condition.'

'For God's sake, Franco, it's hardly a condition! It's not like I'm pregnant!'

'It was a mistake!' he said. 'Now put some damned clothes on and let's get going.'

The scar at his side ached. With cold, Franco told himself, although he knew it was the pain of a thousand mistakes. Sleeping with virgins was right up there on the top of the list. He'd made that mistake once and he damn well wouldn't do it again.

Virgins were needy. They gave up their bodies and then they wanted blood in return. Promises. A lifetime of commitment all tied up with a happily-ever-after bow.

Virgins were trouble.

Michele had never accepted that they shouldn't be together for ever. If she'd come back into his life saying it was just for Nikki, they might even have made a go of it, but she'd taken her daughter's illness and Franco's match as proof that he should never have left her in the first place.

'You were my first,' she'd reminded him constantly. 'You were special.' As if those words would be enough to convince him that he should never have left her behind. Never mind that she hadn't bothered to inform him of her pregnancy or of the child he never knew existed. Never mind their constant fights and the fact that, if it hadn't been for Nikki, they would have never been reunited at all. She would have been nothing more than a part of the history he'd left behind in London, a rebellious fling with a girl he knew his family would never approve of.

A fling that had ended when he'd taken off for Italy to work in the vineyard near Piacenza.

Or so he'd thought.

He rubbed his side.

A twenty-eight-year-old virgin. How was that even possible?

He'd wondered what other surprises Holly Purman was hiding.

But that was one surprise he had not seen coming.

The night was dark and cold and wet, the road a slick ribbon of black, and if it hadn't been framed with white lines, the winding road would have merged into the inky night.

Holly fumed alongside a silent Franco, but if he thought her getting dressed like she'd been told and clambering into the car for the long drive back was going to be an end to the matter, he was going to be sadly mistaken.

The miles added up and so did the tension in the cabin until finally Franco got sick of Holly glaring at him. 'You should try to get some sleep.'

He wished. 'So what's the real reason?'

'What?'

'You said you're not afraid, so what's the real reason you wouldn't make love to me?'

'Dio!' he swore, for it felt like more of a curse when he could say it in Italian. 'Am I going to be subjected to a six-hour interrogation?'

'If that's what it takes.'

He shook his head. 'You're unreal.'

'I'm waiting?'

'You think it will make a difference? That I'll change my mind?'

'I just want to know why you dropped me faster than a hot potato when you found out I was a virgin when you seemed so damned keen up until then. I think that's a fair question to ask, don't you?'

The orange lights of the freeway lit up the interior of the car with a weird otherworldly light. The roads were empty and it was just them and a slick ribbon of freeway and a crazy conversation.

'You won't like it.'

'I'm a big girl, Franco. Hit me with it.'

He looked at her. 'All right. But don't blame me if you don't like what you hear. You take a woman's virginity and you'll always be her first. Good or bad, you'll always be the one against whom all the others are rated. If you're

number two or three or even number ten, you're just another number, but number one, that's special.'

He looked across at her to make sure she was taking
it all in.

'I'm listening.'

'And women get emotional. The first time can hurt,
sometimes a little, sometimes a lot. And then come the
tears and the comforting. And she's already been thinking, Is this the one I'm going to spend my life with, and
now they've shared this amazing experience. Sex compli-
cates that whole thing—when it's her first time, it makes
her want to believe he's the one.'

'And you know this to be fact, of course, as opposed to
some male fantasy of how women work?'

'I've seen it. I'm not making this up.'

'How old was she, Franco? Was she twenty-eight years
old?'

His jaw clenched. 'Sixteen. But it's the same principle.
I'd still be your first.'

'She was a teenager!'

'She was first and foremost a female.'

'And you think I'll get needy.'

'I told you you wouldn't like it.'

'You think I'll start drawing up wedding plans and por-
ing over bridal magazines?'

'I did warn you.'

'Jesus, Franco, there was me thinking you might help
me out with my little problem, and you've got us marching down the aisle.'

'What do you mean?'

'Do you have any idea what it feels like to be a twenty-
eight-year-old virgin? I feel like a freak.'

'So go find someone else to take your virginity out on.
It's not that hard to find someone to sleep with.'

'Maybe not for you. But it is when you grow up in a small town and you know everybody within fifty miles, you know who they talk to in the pub, and you know they talk.'

'It can't be that bad.'

'You want to bet?' She dragged in air, remembering. 'When I was in high school, I confessed to some so-called friends that I'd never had sex. It was all over the school by the end of lunchtime. You know what everyone called me for the rest of the year?'

He looked over at her, shook his head.

'Purman the Virgin. Do you know how many times I heard that during my final year, because I sure lost count?' She sat back in her seat. 'Too many. And if there's one thing I can thank Mark Turner for—that man who was just after the vines as you referred to him—it's that everyone assumed we'd been lovers and they gave up and found somebody else to harass. But if anyone found out now, I'd be a joke all over again. I'd be Purman the Virgin for the rest of my life.

'So no. You can take your needy virgin theory and shove it. Because I wouldn't be your needy virgin wanting to march you down the aisle or have your babies.'

'You don't know that for sure. Sex changes a woman.'

'You think it would change the way I think about you? No, the way I see it, it's foolproof. Because you blow out of here in three weeks' time and we never have to see each other again and I know I'm not going to become the subject of gossip at the local footy club. I know nobody will ever know. And then if I find someone I want to have gratuitous sex with, I can.'

'Who are you thinking of having gratuitous sex with?' he said too quickly. 'Have I met him?'

'That's my secret,' she said with a small smile. 'Maybe

I should have just asked him in the first place.' This time she was rewarded with a glare. 'Maybe I will.'

He grumped into silence, his mood as dark as the night around them. She didn't understand. Didn't want to. Couldn't see past her sad stories and that he might be right.

It was too easy for her. Because she didn't *know*.

He knew.

He'd witnessed a woman tear herself to pieces trying to find an excuse to hang on to a relationship when there was nothing else to hold it together. He'd borne the brunt of her tears and her anguish as she'd tried to find a reason to make the unworkable work.

And all the time he'd known he wasn't blameless.

All the time he'd borne that guilt.

Because from the very beginning he'd let Michele down. He'd used her to get back at his family. He'd used her for his own purposes and then abandoned her just as carelessly when he'd taken off for Italy.

He could use this woman too. No matter what she asked of him, no matter what he agreed to, making love to her would never be an act of generosity. He would take more than he would give. He would be doing it for him. And then, just as he had done to Michele, he would abandon this woman too. He would return to Italy and leave her behind without a backwards glance.

Could he do that again?

Dare he risk it?

Because last time it had cost him a kidney and the love of a child he had known for too short a time.

What would it cost him this time?

She'd called Gus from the car to tell him they'd be home late and she was hoping he'd be tucked up in bed. He wasn't. Gus was waiting for them when they got home, shuffling behind his new walking frame, happy to be out of the wheelchair.

'I hear the highway was blocked for hours this morning,' he said as they pulled boxes from the back of the car to stack on the long table for tomorrow's labelling exercise. 'I'm surprised you didn't stay overnight.'

'We thought about it.'

'Holly was in a hurry to get back,' explained Franco.

'That's funny,' she said, 'I could have sworn that was you.'

They didn't look at each other or at Gus.

'What's that smell?' Gus asked, his nose twitching as they passed. 'You both reek of wine. What happened? Did you drop a bottle?'

'Holly disgorged and dosaged a bottle and forgot to put her thumb over the top.'

Gus frowned and it was clear this was something that had never happened before, anywhere in the annals of Holly Purman wine whisperer folklore. 'Holly forgot?'

'Yeah, Pop,' she said, because it was much, much easier than admitting that Franco had distracted her, and how. 'I forgot.'

CHAPTER TEN

Franco punched his pillow but the pillow fought back and wouldn't let him sleep. He swiped it out from under his head and threw it on the floor, cursing. It wasn't the pillow's fault, he knew that.

It was hers.

Three days they'd been back.

Holly had smiled her way through every one of them as if she hadn't revealed to him her deepest darkest secret. As if she hadn't begged him to make love to her.

Three sleepless nights of reminding himself of all the reasons why he shouldn't go there.

And Holly had taunted him every time he closed his eyes. Holly peeling off her top and revealing those breasts clad in lace and bows. Holly in the shower, with the water cascading over her skin. Holly tasting of wine and woman.

She was killing him. Driving him mad. And she hadn't so much as come near him for days. And whereas in the corking room it had been the brushing against each other, the seemingly casual touches that had stirred him, now it was their lack of touching that stirred him and made him hot with wanting.

And now a new team of workers had arrived to prune the acres of the younger vines and she left him working alone in the old vines to spend half the day with them. He

could hear her laughter welling up from the rows as she
worked alongside them. He could hear their deep voices,
and he wondered if she was thinking about having gratuitous sex with one of them.

And he wondered about his reason for not wanting to
make love to her—a reason that had seemed so potent that
night, but now seemed more feeble by the minute. Shouldn't
her first time be good? Not some fumbled grope in the
dark with someone who didn't care about her experience.

Didn't she deserve a man who knew how to pleasure
a woman?

And it wasn't the same as Michele, surely. Wasn't *she*
taking advantage of *him*—or at least his presence—rather
than the other way around?

And the more he thought about that conversation in the
car, the more he thought maybe she was right. Maybe she
was different. Sure she might be a virgin, but she was older.
She was no Michele—he couldn't imagine her clinging on to
someone after the expiry of their relationship's use-by date.

And Holly's place was very firmly here whereas in a
few short weeks he'd be back to work amongst the rolling hills and vineyards of Piacenza. She wouldn't follow
him. She couldn't without giving up what she'd worked for
here, and there was no way he could see that happening.

Maybe he could help her out, and put a damned stop to
this ceaseless burning.

Maybe he *should* help her out.

Purman the virgin?

Not for much longer.

He growled.

Not if he had anything to do with it.

Mamma Angela's place was buzzing, a huge crowd already gathered by the time Holly arrived with Gus. Ev-

eryone cheered when the guest of honour arrived, proud
that one of their own was a finalist in such a prestigious
award, and Holly beamed. It was a fun party. There was
wine aplenty, as to be expected, freshly pickled local
olives and cheeses all overlaid with the tantalising smell
of a lamb slowly roasting on a spit.

And somewhere amongst the crowd was Franco.

She'd been avoiding him all week, keeping at arm's
length, determined not to look needy. If he truly didn't
want to help her out, he'd welcome the space. On the other
hand, if he was having second thoughts…

Holly didn't know much about seduction, but she hoped
he was having second thoughts.

She found him with Angela overseeing the lamb, the
two rapidly conversing in Italian. Angela wore a big apron
over her button-through dress, her thick black hair curled
back in a ring around her face.

Franco was wearing his sharp Italian threads, the ones
he'd been wearing the first day he'd arrived, complete
with those ridiculously inappropriate hand-stitched loafers.
She'd forgotten how good he'd looked in that outfit—she'd
got so used to seeing him in his bush outfitter gear—but
tonight he was back to European elegance and he looked
more exotic than ever.

He returned her breezy smile with a scowl, and waited
for Angela to throw her arms around Holly and squeeze
her tight before he greeted her. 'Holly.' He nodded, flicking his eyes over her and not looking happy about what
he saw, and she wondered if she'd made a huge blunder
by staying away.

'Franco,' she said uncertainly, 'I'm glad you're here.'

'Of course he come,' Angela said, her hands held out
wide. 'Who else out of this lot outside my family can speak

Italiano. It is so good to speak like my mamma teach me back in Puglia.'

Holly smiled. Clearly Franco had won another fan and she wondered if she'd overblown this whole Chatsfield thing from the start. It wasn't like there'd been anything in the papers for weeks. Maybe even longer...

'And so lucky you are to get him to work in your vineyard. Franco is an expert with the wine.'

'Not as expert as Holly, of course,' he added.

Angela batted that away with one hand. 'But almost as good. I know his family's wines from Piacenza. They are good. You should marry him and start a dynasty.'

It was lucky Holly didn't have a mouthful of wine, or she would have lost it.

Franco was still scowling. But at her, not Angela. What the hell was that about?

'Franco's going home to Italy soon,' she said. 'Aren't you, Franco? So unfortunately it would be a very short-lived dynasty, Angela.'

She shrugged. 'You can't tell young people. Now, this is your party. You go and have fun. I have to see to this lamb.'

They could have headed inside, where the bulk of the partygoers were, but somehow, without a word uttered between them, they drifted instead to a covered pergola area strung with coloured lights, tall gas burners taking the edge off the cold. They stopped at the timber railing and Holly breathed in the air, taking a moment to reflect upon the land that she loved and that had been so good to her. Out there, under the crisp darkness of the night, lay the sleeping vineyards, waiting for spring to wake up and burst once more into life.

But the air she breathed held something more, for it also carried this man's scent and it occurred to her that she would miss it when he was gone.

She sighed, her moment of reflection over, and looked up at him, and whatever was bothering him before must still be bothering him, because he still looked serious.

'Well, you sure look like you're having fun.'

'I'll never understand you, Holly.'

Whoa, was that a compliment or not? She guessed not. 'What's that supposed to mean?'

'You don't know? How about the way you're dressed?'

She looked down at herself. Clean shirt—reasonably pressed pants. She'd even washed her hair and treated herself to a lick of make-up. She thought she looked okay.

He gave a rough, rasping sigh. 'This is a party for you, Holly. A party. All these people are here for you, to celebrate what you have achieved, and you look…' He gazed down at her, a look of utter disbelief on his face. 'You look like you've just come in from a day's pruning in the vineyard. Couldn't you have made an effort?'

Something in her jaw tightened. 'I thought I had.'

'You seem to work extraordinarily hard on making yourself look ordinary.'

She laughed, false. 'Well, I guess it's good to excel at something—'

'That wasn't a compliment, Holly.'

She leaned her elbows down on the railing and turned her gaze out over the dark vineyards. This wasn't going at all the way she'd hoped. 'You're very good at not giving me compliments when it suits you.'

'And I seem to remember you're good at taking them as compliments all the same.'

She shrugged and tightened the grip on her glass of wine. She'd given him space this week, hoping he might come around. But was he still determined to punish her for what had almost happened between them? Was he trying to find fault with everything about her to make himself feel justified?

'Does it really matter what I wear? These people—my friends—are here because I grow good wine. This is what I wear when I grow wine, so why should I pretend to be something I'm not?'

'Because you're a beautiful woman, Holly Purman, and you should stop pretending that you're not. You don't have to hide your beauty under a scraped-back ponytail and a serviceable uniform. What you wear working in the vineyard, for your work, is one thing. What you wear the rest of the time, for the other part of your life, is another. But don't sell yourself short.'

She blinked. Had this man just called her beautiful?

'Why are you so afraid to make something of yourself? What are you scared of—that someone might actually pay you attention? Because you sure do your best to look invisible.'

Did she? She shrugged. 'I've always dressed this way. I grew up practically wearing a Purman's logo somewhere or other. That or a school uniform.'

'Always?'

She remembered the glass of wine in her hands and took a sip. 'I guess Pop didn't know what to do with a girl, especially after Nan died. But he did the best he could, and I guess I was bound to grow up more of a tomboy.'

He thought about what she must have looked like as a little girl, and maybe with pigtails instead of a ponytail, but no doubt much the same. So different from the way Nikki had looked, with her mother's insatiable need to dress her up so she'd looked like a five-year-old going on fifteen, like she'd been her little sister rather than her daughter. He couldn't remember ever seeing her in long pants that weren't tights, come to think of it.

Now he never would.

That old familiar ache stabbed at him again and he shook his head free of thoughts of Nikki. *Dio*, how often had he been reminded of her lately? And this wasn't even about Nikki. This was about a woman who wouldn't be dressed 24/7 in work gear if she was his woman.

'A tomboy with a fetish for lingerie,' he said. 'How does that work exactly?'

And even in the dark he could see her blush. 'I went to a lingerie party once. Reluctantly. And I only bought something because I felt I *should* buy something and it turned out I liked the feel against my skin. I mean, everyone expected me to look the way I did, and shoes and handbags and other girlie things didn't suit the work, but lingerie was pretty and it was my little secret.'

'You know,' he said, his voice softening, 'you wouldn't have this little problem you have if men actually knew what you were wearing underneath.'

She looked up at him and blinked, one long delicious sweep of dark lashes against her cheek, her eyes bold and challenging when she opened them.

'But *you* know, and I've still got "this little problem."'

Touché. But not for long.

He put his hand to her face and drew the back of his fingers down her cheek and felt her shuddering response. 'I need to admit something to you, Holly. There's another reason I want to see you dressed in silk. A selfish reason. And that's because when I dream about making love to you, I dream about peeling a gown made from silk from your skin and letting it pool at your feet, rather than unbuttoning you out of your khaki armour plating and work boots.'

'You dream about undressing me?' Pink tongue moistened pink lips. Her breath caught.

He nodded. 'But it looks like, in this case, I'll just have to make an exception.'

Her heart skipped a beat.

'Does that mean…?' she whispered, hardly daring to hope. 'Are you saying that…?'

'I'm saying that I'll make love to you, Holly. I'm volunteering to help you out with your little problem. I'll show you how good it can be making love to a man. But that's all I'm promising. Nothing more.'

She blinked up at him and whispered, 'Yes,' and he longed to pull her into his arms and show her just how much he wanted to, but they weren't exactly alone and they didn't need to make this arrangement public. She didn't need the baggage of people whispering after he'd left that she'd been abandoned for the second time by someone who only wanted her for the vines. So instead he blocked her from view with his body, and allowed himself the sweet luxury of tracing the curve of her lip with one finger.

'That was the right answer.'

She opened her mouth and caught the tip of it between her pink lips and brushed it with the tip of her tongue and he felt his groin tighten so hard it would take a solid ten minutes of walking in a cold vineyard before he could rejoin the party.

The party seemed interminable, and while Gus begged off relatively early after the speeches, the guest of honour could hardly leave before the end. And the party was wonderful, Mamma Angela's lamb on the spit was sublime and people were genuinely excited for Holly, the entire community behind her, and not just because a win for Holly was a win for the entire region.

But while on the outside she smiled and accepted their congratulations, on the inside she burned.

Because Franco would make love to her.
Tonight.

She'd behaved herself all night, sitting on one glass of wine because this was her party and she was the guest of honour and she couldn't let herself get messy.

Or that's how it had started.

Then she'd been too wired to drink, too conscious that every passing minute took her one minute closer to the afterparty, the private party to come between her and Franco.

But being stone cold sober had its disadvantages too, when it meant you were tense and jumpy and your throat scratchy and dry, and as Franco held open the car door for her and she gave him a tight smile, Holly wished she'd had a couple more.

Never was a bottle of Purman's Rubida on a back seat a more welcome sight.

'I see you brought us something to drink,' she said as he climbed into the driver's seat, and he just smiled enigmatically.

'You could say that.'

'I thought it best to use the cottage,' he said as he pulled up outside. 'Less chance of you being recognised than if we turned up at a hotel anywhere around here.'

She nodded. Thank God one of them was thinking. She'd been too busy anticipating. 'What about Josh?'

'Josh is "otherwise engaged" with the girl from the bakery. He won't be back before lunch tomorrow.'

'Really?' Josh and Rachel? God, was everyone in the world having sex but her?

Which reminded her...

'I guess, you have...erm...' Oh, God, she could feel herself going red.

'Protection?'

'Yeah.'

'Of course.'

She felt so naive. So inexperienced. A man like Franco Chatsfield probably didn't leave home without condoms. And that thought didn't bear thinking about so she just smiled weakly and pushed the loose strands of hair back behind her ears while Franco rounded the car to open her door. Then her door was open and Franco offered his hand and his eyes were smouldering and there was no turning back.

Oh, boy.

Around them vines slumbered on their wires under an ink-blue night sky while gum leaves scarcely shivered on the soft breeze. It was like the whole world was holding its breath.

'It was a great party, wasn't it?' Holly said, needing to fill the silence.

'And everyone was so happy for me,' she babbled as they made their way down the path. 'It seemed like everyone from the district was there.'

He unlocked the door and she walked inside, still spilling words. 'And that lamb! Oh, my God, how good was that lamb!'

'Holly,' he said, snapping on the heater and putting the wine in the fridge.

'And did you get to try one of Angela's olives? Only she does the best olives. Brought the recipe with her from Puglia. It was her grandmother's and her grandmother's before that.'

'Holly,' he said again, reaching for her hand.

'Yes?'

He spun her hard against him. 'Shut up.' His mouth silenced hers with a kiss that started at her lips and went all the way down. His mouth was hot, his body hard, and she knew when to argue and when to take advice. And right now was no time to argue.

The man knew how to kiss. God knows how many women he'd practised his technique upon, or how many tutors he'd learned from along the way, but he was expert, very expert. And that tongue? That tongue was so wicked it should come with a government health warning.

It lured hers into the dance, of breath and mouth and lips and tongue, a dance between two, a dance with one purpose. One end.

She joined the dance, of breath and mouth and lips and tongue, and danced with him, craving that end. Needing it.

And his hands moulded her to him, one hand in the small of her back, the other on her behind, so they were connected chest to chest, thigh to thigh, length to length. And she ached, knowing that still it wasn't close enough.

They wouldn't be close enough until he was inside her.

And she needed more than anything for him to be inside her.

Now.

His mouth still making magic on hers, she splayed the fingers of one hand on his chest and moved them slowly south, over the hard-packed chest, to his well-formed abdomen, to the bulge that ridged his fine Italian trousers, and he growled into her mouth.

'Please?' she whimpered back, because she didn't know how else to show her desperation. 'Please?'

He blinked down at her, a smile tugging at the corners of his lips. 'Didn't you ever hear, Holly, that patience is a virtue?'

'Patience is overrated.'

His face grew serious as he drew circles on her cheek with his thumb. 'Fast isn't good, Holly, not the first time.'

And Holly pressed her lips together because it was the wrong answer.

'Why don't you get into bed,' he suggested, 'while I get the wine?'

She nodded, teeth gnawing at her lip. It would be progress of sorts.

He put a finger to her lips to stop her teeth. 'I'll be right back.'

She wasted no time kicking off her shoes and peeling off her shirt and pants, sliding between sheets bearing delicious Franco's scent, and anticipation ratcheted up yet another notch.

She sure needed that wine.

She heard the pop of the cork and the fizz of rushing wine and her nerves built to fever pitch and then he was there, bearing two flutes filled with the golden liquid. He sat down on the bed beside her and she scooted up as he handed her a glass.

'Here's to Holly Purman,' he said, 'soon to be ex-virgin.' She laughed nervously and took a sip and then another. Perfect. And he took her glass away, put them both on the side table and leaned over and kissed her on the mouth. 'Mmm,' he murmured, 'vintage Holly,' and then, still kissing her, dispensed with shoes and trousers and his chest-hugging sweater.

He straightened only to peel down that band of black and she watched as he swung free, magnificent and proud, and she fizzed like that wine at the thought of him inside her. 'You're beautiful,' she said, and he smiled as he peeled back the covers from her chest, his hungry eyes feasting on her breasts dressed in a soft pink-and-white-striped bra. His erection twitched.

'That's my line,' he said, his thumb tracing the line where fabric met flesh. 'I'm so glad you left these on,' he said. 'Maybe it's not a silk gown, but I'll enjoy peeling these from your body.' He eased the straps down, peeling down the cups of her bra until it was his hands around her breasts, his thumbs stroking her nipples until she mewled with pleasure. One hand circled under her back and a moment later the bra was gone. His hands skimmed down her sides, moulding to the curve of her waist and the flare of her hips, and as they travelled down, he caught his thumbs in the matching candy-striped underwear and groaned as he peeled it down her legs.

'Holly, you are so beautiful.' He leaned down to kiss her, his hand stroking her from her shoulder to her knee, and it was so intoxicating, so magical to her senses, that she barely noticed when he reached for his wine.

She felt the dribble against her lips, recognised it for what it was and felt his hot mouth lapping at hers, their tongues tangling, sharing the wine.

A drop landed on her chest, and she gasped, but he was there to lap it up before it could slide away. Another on a nipple, his tongue curling to chase the wine, drawing her nipple into his mouth and sending spears of sensation between her thighs where she could feel the pulsing, aching heat.

Her other nipple demanded the same, received the same, and Holly pushed her head back into the pillows and arched into his mouth.

A line of drops down her belly and Holly sensed where this was going. He didn't need to. They'd done that. There was no point—

And then she felt him part her, felt the cool slide of wine against her hot flesh and his hot tongue and need spiralled within her and it was a battle to stay afloat. She didn't want to come this way because she'd already come this way, but neither could she stop as sensation piled upon sensation until it seemed there was nowhere else to go.

Her fingers clung to his head as fingers stroked that aching place, massaging, loosening, as his mouth played her. She felt the slide of his finger inside her, and then another, felt their play against her inner flesh and a coiling need turned incendiary and consumed her in a roaring whoosh of flame.

She heard a rip and a tear but she was still coming down when she felt the press of him there, still too drugged and dazed and spent to tense and fear, even when he nudged at her entrance. She just felt the pressure at her core and she wanted it and welcomed it and angled her hips to meet him, and with a blinding flicker of pain that had her cry out, he was inside her, holding still, waiting.

He kissed her lightly on the mouth. 'Are you all right?'

And she nodded because she was, and it was strange, this new sensation, of muscles shifting and making way, of feeling his long slow slide into her body until he was buried to the hilt inside her.

Better than okay.

Because now there was a delicious friction. Flesh against slick flesh, and new-found muscles to experiment with and increase the friction. And she wouldn't have thought it possible—hadn't she only just climaxed?—but this was different, this build-up was coming from inside, and building with every long slide. She clung to him as he increased the tempo, needing a rock to hold her steady while sensation built upon sensation and threatened to carry her away. But there was no escaping, no place to hide, as he took her higher, the exquisite pressure building to fever pitch as he took a nipple between his teeth as he thrust into her, and it was all she needed to go hurtling over the edge once again.

It took a while to come back to earth, for her breathing to slow, for her heart rate to calm, but still her flesh hummed and her mind buzzed with the sheer wonderment of what had just happened.

'Thank you,' she said to the man who lay sweat-slicked, his skin glistening, at her side. 'That was very nice.'

He opened a pair of sex-drugged eyes. 'Do you feel any different?'

'Yes, I do. I feel—' she sucked in air '—amazing!'

He curved one hand around a breast. 'That you do.'

'Do you think…' she ventured. 'Is there any chance we could do it again?'

His slumbering cock woke up with a jolt, but he wasn't so sure. It would no doubt be mind-blowing, as before, but there was danger here too, he recognised. He didn't want her thinking this meant anything.

His every instinct told him to pull back now.

'Do you think that's wise? Your little problem has now been taken care of, so you don't actually need me. You can go have sex with anyone you like and nobody will ever know.' Although why that thought didn't make him any happier, he didn't know.

'Yeah,' she said, running her fingers through the spring of hair on his chest, 'but I can hardly call myself experienced. There's more to learn, I know there is. And you're only here a couple more weeks anyway. Why shouldn't we take advantage? I won't tell if you won't.'

He shook his head. He really should get her up and dressed and drop her home.

'It's madness, Holly. You've had sex. You're no longer a virgin. That was the deal.'

'Only that thing you did with the wine…' she ventured.

Dio, he shouldn't ask. He knew he shouldn't. 'What about it?'

'I'd really like to try that on you.'

And his growing erection twitched and bucked and he knew he was lost.

Hours later he woke with her in his arms. Soon, he knew, the grey fingers of dawn would work their way through the curtains. The night had been long and full of the pleasures of the flesh and he knew he had to get her back to the house. It was madness that she was still here. But she was warm and relaxed in his arms and he thought, just a few minutes more.

And then she stirred and stretched and he pulled her in tight against him, pressing his lips to her hair, and she responded by turning in his arms and winding her arms around his neck. He felt her breasts against his chest and the curl of her hair against his belly and it was enough to stir his half-ready body again.

'Are you hurting?' he asked.

'I feel wonderful,' she said against his mouth, and he felt her smile on his lips. 'I feel like I've been liberated from what was starting to feel like a life sentence. Thank you.'

'It was my pleasure,' he said, his own smile on his lips when they met hers. One of her hands skimmed down his side, hesitating at that raised cord of scar tissue, and he stiffened, waiting for the question he knew was coming.

'What is this?'

'Nothing,' he answered, the way he always did.

'Were you in a car crash?'

'No.'

'Then—'

'Dammit, Holly,' he said, shoving back the covers as he strode from the bed, any sense of wellbeing demolished. They'd shared great sex, sure, but that didn't mean she had to know the intimate details of his life. His private life was private and he intended to keep it that way. She was temporary. Whereas his scar—his reminder—was permanent. 'Does it matter?'

'I was just asking.'

'It's time I took you home.'

'Fine,' she said, collecting up underwear and shimmying into it coyly in the bed like he hadn't already explored every inch of her naked body. Women were mad, he thought, pulling on his trousers. 'I just don't know why it's such a big deal.'

And the control he'd once prided himself on, the control he'd found sorely tested ever since he'd turned up and met prickly Ms Purman, threatened to blow.

'I donated a kidney to—' *my five-year-old daughter* '—a friend. That's all. End of story. Satisfied?'

She looked up at him in the watery light of predawn. 'That's all? But that's an amazing thing to do.'

His lips pulled tight into a grimace and he shook his head. 'It might have been,' he said, as empty as the day she'd left them. 'If she'd made it.'

'Oh, Franco. I'm so sorry.'

'Don't be,' he said, pulling his jumper over his head, wishing he'd taken her home after the first time they'd made love like he'd intended. Like he should have and would have if he hadn't been blindsided by sex. 'It wasn't your fault.'

He pulled on shoes and his jacket and grabbed his keys, wondering how it was that every time they talked she seemed to remind him of his mother or his siblings or his daughter, always dredging up the past, always digging up things he wanted to stay buried. 'Are you coming?'

She lay unsleeping on her bed in the short space between dawn and morning proper, after twenty-eight years, no longer a virgin. She wouldn't go back in a heartbeat, not after the pleasures Franco had introduced her to this night.

She clutched the sheets around her chest. She would never forget this night. She would never forget Franco. She just wished it hadn't ended so badly. He'd dropped her home with barely a word, his chiselled jaw rigid, his grey eyes as cold as the clouds that dropped icy fat drops on her as she ran inside.

He was hurting. He'd tried to make out that his scar meant nothing, but she'd felt his pain in the struggle he'd had to even acknowledge it.

He'd donated a kidney to a friend. He'd given a part of himself to another. What kind of man did that? Not the kind of man she'd thought Franco to be when he'd blown into her world those few short weeks ago. He wasn't that man. He was so much more.

And he was hurting, his friend lost, no matter the sacrifice he'd made, his scar a constant reminder.

Of course he would be hurting.

And she lay in her bed and ached for a man who wasn't hers to ache for.

His hip ached. He rolled over in bed but his hip still ached. He lay on his back and still his hip ached. So in the end, sick of thrashing, he got out of bed and stood by the window in the living room. The cool air would soothe his scar, he told himself, his eyes glued to the flicker of light from the homestead across the vineyard.

She was over there. No doubt tucked up in bed and sleeping peacefully now that she'd finally rid herself of that pesky virgin status.

Now that he'd rid her of that pesky virgin status.

So what was his problem? Why couldn't he sleep? He'd

had the best sex he'd had for as long as he could remember. He should be sleeping like a baby.

Across the vineyard the light danced and shimmied in the cold night air, and if he didn't know better, he'd think it was meant solely for him, the silent equivalent of the kookaburra's laugh.

Because it hadn't been just sex.

With Holly it had never been just about having sex.

Tonight they'd made love.

Air sucked through teeth and rushed into his lungs. How the hell had he let things go so wrong when he'd known the dangers all along? Why hadn't she listened to him and stayed well away?

Why hadn't he had the strength of will to resist her?

The lights of the homestead flickered gaily across the darkness, mocking him and mocking all the reasons he'd given her why they shouldn't have sex.

Because he'd been her first.

Because she might become needy.

And yet here he was, standing at a window across a vineyard looking over to where she lay safely tucked up inside. Because when it came to Holly Purman, no matter what he knew or what he'd learned, he had no strength to resist her.

Who was the needy one now?

Which made the next few weeks hell unless he learned to stay away from her.

And the scar at his hip, knowing that was impossible, ached worse than ever.

CHAPTER ELEVEN

'But, Pop, you have to be there! You can't miss it. This is your night, just as much as it is mine.'

'I'd love to go, Holly,' he said, and she could see the dampness in his eyes and the stoic way he kept the tears in check. 'I wish I could go, but it's my own bloody fault. If I hadn't been trying to do too much and fallen over and buggered up all the good work the doctors had done I could go. But if the doctors tell me they won't let me on a plane, then what choice do I have? I can't go.'

'I don't want to go by myself.'

'You have to. It's your night. You'll just have to get Franco to go with you.'

A weekend alone in Sydney with Franco. Franco hadn't made so much as a move towards her since the night of the party, and Holly couldn't pretend the idea wasn't without appeal. 'But, Pop…'

'Don't "But, Pop" me. I've seen the way you look at him, don't think I haven't. You like him, don't you?'

She shrugged. 'He's…okay. It's worked out better than I thought it would. Given he's a Chatsfield, I mean.'

Gus chuckled. 'Don't lay it on too thick or I'll change my mind. Are you glad now I didn't let you throw him out on his ear that first day? You sure tried your hardest.'

Was she glad? Definitely in one way. Because she'd

learned so much these past weeks from the perils of pre-judging to the pleasures of the flesh. And she'd learned so much about herself into the deal.

Then again, maybe it would have been easier if he'd left that day and she'd never seen him again. Because thinking about watching him walk out of her life when the pruning was finished gave her a dull empty ache in her chest. She would miss him when he was gone.

'I do feel better about the wine deal now.' And that had nothing to do with Franco, for the Chatsfield siblings seemed to have kept themselves out of the scandal sheets for long enough that it looked like the wine deal may not be the disaster she'd first feared.

Besides, signing the deal meant there was always a chance of seeing Franco in the future.

She wasn't needy. Truly she wasn't, but she wouldn't object if their paths were to cross again.

'Go on then,' Gus said, 'take Franco to Sydney instead of me. Show him the sights and have some fun. And when you win, it might well be a good chance maybe to get some publicity about the deal.'

'*If* I win, Pop.'

'My money's on you, my girl. That award is as good as yours.'

They were in the vineyard together when she asked him.

'I'll come,' Franco said, albeit warily, 'if that's what Gus wants.' Since the night of the party he'd kept his distance, but to her credit, Holly had too, and he'd wondered whether she'd been right when she'd told him she wasn't the needy type. But while he'd kept his distance, it hadn't stopped him wanting her. He told himself he had no choice, that maybe they might still renege on signing the contract if he didn't agree, but selfishly he knew that keeping his distance was killing him, and that a weekend in Sydney could be mutually beneficial. There was still more he could teach her, he told himself, if she wanted. 'But I'll have to get a suit. What are you wearing?'

She sucked air between her teeth. 'That's just it. I don't have anything yet.'

He smiled at that, in spite of the anticipation growing in his loins. 'Of course you don't.'

'I was planning on going into the Mount tomorrow and having a look.'

'Into Mount Gambier?' He swore under his breath in his mother's tongue. He was doing a bit of that lately, but then he had good cause this time.

'I heard there's a sale on at Betty's Drapery. I thought I'd check it out tomorrow.'

'A sale. At Betty's Drapery. You do realise this function is at the Opera House and that you may very well win and you will be going up on a podium to speak and you will be filmed and photographed a thousand times from a thousand different angles.'

He saw her blanch, watched her throat constrict as she swallowed. 'This dress is going to have to be something extraordinary, and you think you'll find it at Betty's on a sale rack?'

She balled her fists, tears squeezing from her eyes. 'I hate this. Why does everything have to be so complicated? I just want to grow my grapes and make my wine and now this has to happen and what am I going to do?'

'Simple,' he said. 'Go to Betty's if you must, and buy yourself something to wear on the plane that isn't khaki, and then we'll find you a decent dress in Sydney.'

He'd changed their flights to two days earlier to give them time to go shopping. And now she watched the changing view of the cliffs and coastline as their plane circled before landing in Sydney. Today the city was bathed in sunshine, the Sydney Harbour Bridge and Opera House, iconic features of the beautiful harbour, standing proud.

She didn't really think it could take two days to find one suit and a dress, but clearly she didn't know a whole lot about shopping for major events and it was nice to let Franco take charge of this part of the arrangements. She was nervous enough about Saturday as it was without worrying about anything else.

First would come the pre-dinner drinks, where the six finalists were all introduced to the guests and each had a few minutes to talk about their inspiration, their influences and their vision. Holly's speech was a lot about Gus. She figured it was the only chance she'd get to speak and she wanted him to be recognised when he'd done so much to shape her into the winemaker she was, especially when he couldn't be there in person.

Then on to the formal dinner before the announcement of the winner at nine after which they would thankfully go home and life would return to normal.

Or not quite normal in her case.

She wasn't sure it would ever be normal again.

There was a car waiting for them outside arrivals. A red one, with bright red duco and gleaming chrome. She just looked at it and laughed. 'A Maserati? You actually got a Maserati?'

'What choice did I have? They were all out of helicopters.'

She smiled up at him as he held open the door for her. 'I just hate it when that happens.'

Whoa, she thought as he manoeuvred the beast into the Sydney traffic. And not only because of the acceleration.

But because for a moment there she'd felt a connection, a thread of shared experiences that made for a private joke.

An insanely expensive private joke.

'Have you got a licence to drive this thing?'

'Relax, I'm half Italian. It's in the blood.'

Maybe it was, she thought as she breathed in air flavoured with the unfamiliar taste of the big smoke, and relaxed back in her seat. Right now she was here in Sydney with this gorgeous man in this audacious car and she was going to enjoy it.

She watched him as he relished being in control of this monster, putting on a burst of acceleration to squeeze into a gap in the next lane with apparent ease. She didn't want to think about how much the insurance excess was on this baby, but he seemed totally relaxed. But then, he was made for driving a car like this, or maybe a car like this was designed to surround a man like him—European design, at its core wild and untamed, all wrapped up in a civilised—if very sexy—package.

Even the way he handled the streets in a foreign city had her impressed. The Coonawarra could get busy, sure, on festival weekends or in peak season, but this was workaday madness and it just went on and on.

'How do you know where you're going?'

'Sheer gut instinct,' he answered, looking so superbly confident behind the wheel that she almost believed him. Then he looked at her over his sunglasses. 'And I may have checked a map. It's not that hard. Not far now.'

And while she loved the playfulness he sometimes showed, she almost wished he'd never given a glimpse of this side of his character. It made it harder to remember this was temporary. It made it too easy to wish for things that she shouldn't wish for, things that could never be.

She gazed out at the busy city streets, the swirling traffic and the crush of pedestrians, promising herself that she would not fall into that trap. She'd sworn black and blue that she wouldn't get emotional or needy or start thinking domestic bliss. And yet here she was already dreading his leaving. Knowing she would miss him. Knowing it would hurt.

Two weeks, that was all they probably had left together, given the progress they'd made with the pruning. Two short weeks at most.

That was all she was ever going to have.

She tossed her hair back and took a deep, settling breath.

It would be enough.

It would have to be.

He took a right at an intersection and pulled into a hotel reception driveway. 'Here we are.'

'The Chatsfield? But I thought—'

'I changed the reservation,' he said.

'Why?'

'I get a family discount.' And he shot her a smile that made her laugh as the doorman opened her door and welcomed her to the hotel.

But really, the Chatsfield?

'My parents were married here,' she mused, taking in the classical facade of the stone building as he handed over the car key to the valet and joined her.

'I know,' he said, serious again. 'I hope you don't mind. I thought you might want to see.'

'No, it's...lovely. It's so strange to think of them here so many years ago.'

'I've got something to show you. Once we're all checked in.'

All she could do was nod and smile as the brass-framed glass door opened into the smiling luxurious world of Sydney's version of the Chatsfield.

It was like stepping back in time, Holly thought as she passed through the marble entry, although it wasn't old-fashioned so much as classically elegant. Nothing looked cheap. Nothing looked shabby. Even the city air had been left behind and there was a note on the air—lemongrass?—clean and fresh. The whole impression was quality all the way, like she'd imagined Chatsfield's had been in the past, before its reputation had been tarnished.

This hotel didn't look tarnished.

Check-in was awesomely efficient. Amazing, of course, what a Chatsfield name on the booking could do to speed that up. And then they were shown to their room.

No, make that suite.

A suite with a view.

'Our finest suite,' said their well-practised personal concierge, who pushed open the door to a view that anyone in their right mind would gladly pay millions for and probably did. The best of Sydney was spread out around them with a panorama that stretched from the Sydney heads on one side all the way to the sails of the Opera House and the Harbour Bridge on the other.

He gave them a second to drink in the view before showing them around their extravagant suite, a king-size bedroom complete with four-poster bed, a sumptuous marble bathroom and the expansive lounge area complete with dining table and where fresh flowers filled vases on timber side tables, lending their sweetness to the air.

'A beautiful city,' Franco said beside her after the concierge had left and they returned to the windows overlooking the city.

Holly was awestruck. She was actually here, in Sydney, looking out over a diamond-tipped harbour dotted with ferries and yachts criss-crossing the waters. And there, nestled alongside the harbour, was the Opera House, where

Saturday's award presentation would be made. All of a sudden she felt ill. She put a hand to her stomach, where butterflies were madly flapping their wings. 'I don't think I'm ready for this,' she said.

'You will be,' he assured her, and then, 'Come with me, there's something I want you to see.'

He took her down the lift to the library room, a sumptuously rich dark room with panelled timber walls and high ceilings and shelves filled with books and old leather-bound ledgers. Wing-backed chairs and low tables strewn with the day's newspapers from around the globe invited one to sit down and linger.

'A lot of the archival material for the hotel is kept in here,' he told her, 'but this,' he said, leading her towards a timber-and-glass cabinet on one wall between shelves, 'is what I wanted you to see.'

And as she came closer she saw. There was a dried flower arrangement and an assortment of papers and newspaper clippings and above it all a photograph, of a smiling bride and groom holding a knife poised over a beautiful three-tier wedding cake.

Her parents.

Her mother in the beautiful white dress that she'd seen in the old newspaper cutting, but unlike the cutting, this picture was clear and crisp and she could see the piping on the dress and the lace at her neck and the tiny buttons on the cuffs of her sleeves.

The entire contents of the cabinet were given over to a record of that day on the Chatsfield Sydney's opening weekend, complete with copies of the menu of their wedding breakfast and an order of ceremony.

And the flowers? Holly gasped as she read the note printed alongside. Holly's mother's bouquet, which her mother had offered to the hotel as thanks for their perfect wedding.

And it was so beautifully preserved, the roses crinkled at the edges but still pink, the tiny white gypsophila sprigs still light as air between.

Her mother had held this walking down the aisle to meet her father.

She pored over each and every item, read each little card at least twice, not wanting to miss a single tiny detail, and as she drank it all in, she realised she'd been given a gift—a glimpse of her parents on their special day as they'd started their new family together.

She sniffed, bit her lips together so she didn't do more. 'Thank you,' she said, 'it's beautiful.'

'I thought you'd like to see it.'

She couldn't pretend any more. She brushed away the tears on her cheeks.

'How did you know this was here?'

'I didn't, not really, but I guessed there would be some record kept, at least a picture. I contacted the manager and he told me of this cabinet and its contents. They want to get a photograph of you next to it, if you agree.'

'Of course,' she said, having to bite her lips together once again. 'Gus would especially love to see it, I know.

'Thank you,' she said, smiling tremulously up at this man who had found this for her and made it possible.

She looked so vulnerable—so lonely—so alone. She was smiling but not with any great conviction and his first thought was to hold her. To comfort her for her loss. Strange, they were both without family. All she had now was Gus. He had no one really.

But then he'd chosen to walk away from his family.

She'd never had a choice to begin with.

He felt her hand in his, her other on his arm as she

squeezed both of them tightly. 'Thank you.' And what choice did he have but to put his other arm around her and hug her to his chest after all? What power could stop him?

Even if he knew it was madness.

Even if he knew it was for nothing.

Because he could never be someone's comfort or strength ever again, and the last thing he needed to do was let this woman think he could.

No wonder Franco had balked at the likes of Betty's Drapery. Because while Holly didn't have much of an idea about shopping generally, Franco's concept of going shopping might as well have been on a different planet.

For a start, they didn't actually go shopping. The shopping came to them.

'How did you do this?' she asked as a slimline keen-eyed madame and her similarly attired younger assistants rapidly turned the suite's living room into a boutique. And if the older woman reminded her of a girls' high school principal—with lashings more make-up—the younger women were like unsmiling head prefects—tall and willowy slim and who knew their hallowed place in the world.

'I made a call. I don't know where to shop in Sydney, so I had someone listen to what I needed and take it from there.'

'I don't see any suits.' Although there were plenty of gowns, boxes of shoes, cartons of lingerie and evening bags. 'What are you going to do?'

'I'll go shopping tomorrow.'

'What will I do tomorrow?'

'You'll be busy enough. You'll be in the day spa.'

Before she could tell him she hardly needed an entire day to have a bath, the high school principal—who'd introduced herself as 'Penelope, please don't call me

Penny'—bustled over to claim and transform her latest fashion victim.

'Now, what do we have to work with here?' She took Holly's chin in her hand and held her face up to the light. 'Hmm, good skin, though could clearly do with some help.' And to Holly, 'Stay out of the sun, dear, it'll turn your skin to crocodile hide.'

She caught Franco's smile under his hand and glared at him.

'Green eyes. No, let me see—' she twisted her face some more '—more like turquoise. Hmm, interesting. Blonde hair—could go a bit blonder. Needs highlights— no, low lights, I think. Note that down for the salon.' And then she stepped back to take all of her in. 'Size...ten. Eight possibly, but those curves...' She shook her head as she stood back to consider Holly's hips and breasts. 'No. Let's not be too positive. Let's start with size ten and see how we go. We don't want to be disappointed, do we? All right, girls, bring me...' And Queen Penelope issued a stream of instructions that had her princesses running around in their perfectly high heels.

'I'll leave you to it,' said Franco, despite the fact he was looking altogether too much like he was enjoying this, and leaving Holly to the clutches of the woman and her help- ers as she was undressed and redressed and her hair tied up this way and that and she was ordered to swivel and parade while walking on stilts.

Not a high school principal at all, Holly reconsidered as she watched her wield her power, mostly over her. Penel- ope was more a high priestess of fashion and her assistants, her vestal virgins, priestesses in training.

She wondered what they'd have thought if she'd turned up in her usual Purman Wines attire.

Although maybe that would have been a bridge too far.

It took the best part of two hours. Coffee, water and pastries had to be sent for twice. The women bolted down the coffee and sniffed at the pastries and merely sighed. Holly reached for a pastry at one time to be met with a collective gasp. She reached for the water instead.

But finally they seemed happy. They stood in a circle around her, examining her for any flaw, any bulge. There couldn't possibly be anything bulging, Holly figured, not with the industrial-strength restraining device they'd shoehorned her into that seemed to squeeze all her organs into the space air once took in her lungs. Which probably explained why she was finding it so difficult to breathe.

'Well?' the high priestess asked of her coven. 'What do we think? What is our verdict?'

Definitely queen speak, Holly thought, amending the call once again.

'I like it,' said one, and Holly would have sighed with relief if only she could breathe.

'The colour is perfect,' said another, 'for those eyes.' This time Holly found a smile.

'And it does wonders for her figure,' said a third. Holly ignored her. That was probably all down to the boa constrictor she had on underneath anyway. 'I think it's the one.'

'Done!' the high priestess declared. 'That's settled then. Pack up, girls.'

Holly blinked. 'Do I get a horse in this race?'

'Excuse me?'

'Do I get to have a look in the mirror and see if *I* like it?'

Apparently nobody had ever asked Penelope this question before. 'If you must,' she agreed, appalled that her authority might be questioned. A cheval mirror was found and duly wheeled up, and the head priestess sniffed again. 'Of course, you have to imagine it with your hair and make-up professionally done. At the moment you look quite underdone in it, so you'll have to make allowances.'

Holly was only too happy to agree to those terms. She just hoped she liked it or there'd clearly be hell to pay.

She looked at herself as the mirror was adjusted from side to side, looked at the reflection staring back at her and wondered what miracle had been performed that she, grape-wrangler from the Coonawarra, could be transformed into a fairytale princess.

The dress was one-shouldered, with a diamante clasp over the collarbone that sparkled like diamonds when she moved the slightest fraction, and it skimmed over her breasts to a cinched-in waist, while the skirt seemed inspired by the ancient Greeks, the fabric draped to fit elegantly but not in the least way cling.

But the best thing was the colour. It was the exact turquoise of her eyes and even 'underdone' as she was they seemed to glow with it.

'Well?' snipped Penelope-don't-call-me-Penny behind her, back in pen-tapping headmistress mode.

'I love it,' she said. 'I can't believe it's me.'

Penelope sniffed and scratched an imaginary itch behind her ear. A physical 'go figure.' 'And now we can pack up, girls.'

And with the destructive force of a cyclone they set about doing just that, packing away shoes into crates and dresses onto racks to be wheeled away by the porters while Holly was left to get changed in her own time.

She didn't rush. She stood in the bedroom staring into the mirror for a while after they had gone, thinking about a girl who had grown up more like a boy and who had never once thought she might have reason to look like this, even if it were ever possible she could.

She thought about a man who hired helicopters and

Maseratis like other people hired a power tool, and who knew how to find someone who could turn tomboys into Cinderellas.

And she wondered if it were possible...

But then she shook her head free of such thoughts as she stepped from the gown and struggled her way free of the clutches of the boa constrictor beneath. It didn't pay to wonder.

'How was the shopping?' Franco asked half an hour later when he returned with a package in his hands.

'No good,' she said with a thumbs-down from the sofa where she was reading up on her competition for the award. Some of them she already knew or had heard of, but reading their bios had made all of them depressingly good. Depressingly deserving. The dress might well turn out to be a complete waste of money. Unless they decided to award a prize for best-dressed female. Given she was the only female amongst the six, she was at least in the running for that one. 'What's in the box?' she said, and Franco looked at it, frowning.

'Just that koala picture. I had it framed. But hang on...' he said, his expression bubbling over from surprise to annoyance, and she could see the pressure building in his grey eyes. *Excellent.* 'What happened?' he demanded, right on cue.

She shrugged and tossed the magazine away. 'The woman simply had no clue about fashion. So I've decided to use the gown I bought the other day at Betty's Drapery, just in case I couldn't find a thing to wear in Sydney.'

It took him all of a split second to realise she was joking. It took another split second for her to be scooped in his arms and whirled around, giggling, towards the bedroom. 'Don't mess with me,' he warned.

'Or what?' she said provocatively, already wending her fingers through his gorgeous wavy hair, tingling all over because she already knew the answer to her question.

'Or you'll pay for it.'

She smiled up at him as he tumbled her on the big four-poster bed. 'I was hoping you'd say that.'

CHAPTER TWELVE

IF HEDONISM MEANT the pursuit of pleasure, Holly idly thought as the warm stones were strategically placed on her well-oiled back, then the receiving of pleasure must be the definition of day spa.

The pleasure had begun the moment she'd walked through the doors of Chatsfield's Lotus Harmony Day Spa and relaxed with a cup of fragrant tea.

Since then she'd been pampered and oiled by angels in soft pink uniforms with gentle voices and even gentler hands. They'd massaged every inch of her body until she tingled all over and now she had stones.

Oh, God, it was so relaxing.

And it didn't end there because next up was the hairdresser and a new style and colour after which Franco had promised to take her to dinner.

She couldn't remember another time when she'd felt so spoiled and pampered.

A girl could get used to this.

Then again, she thought, thinking more wisely this time, a girl better not.

He lay in bed, listening to the breathing of the woman in his arms and feeling more heartsick with every slow breath. They'd dined on seafood tonight, the best Sydney had to offer, and then they'd taken a walk along a sandy beach where the sea provided the music in the crash and shoosh of waves on shore. Then they'd come back to the hotel and made love long into the night.

And that was half the problem. He'd recognised the danger—he'd known where this would lead—and yet still he'd talked himself into believing he could enjoy a few more nights of instruction, of passing on what he knew, and then simply walk away.

And now a one-night stand—a favour—had gone to spending the night in the same bed and waking up together in each other's arms.

His gut told him he was headed for a fall.

Too restless to sleep, he eased his arm out from under her neck. She stirred and muttered an unintelligible protest and slipped back into sleep the moment her head was back on the pillow.

He padded to the windows and looked out—the city of Sydney lay dressed up for the night in lights of every colour and the harbour shone silver under a fat moon.

He was a fool. He should have done what she'd asked. Relieved her of her virginity. And then walked away.

Wrong.

He should have left her well alone, because this was always bound to happen.

He'd seen the looks she'd given him when she thought he wasn't looking. The longing. The need.

And now she expected to curl against him and sleep with her head upon his shoulder. It didn't matter that for that first moment when he woke, with her warm body in his arms and her head curled against his shoulder and her breath softly fanning his chest, that he might wish for something more.

Because there could be no more.

And the longer it went on, the worse it would get, and the ache in his hip would never go away.

He so needed that ache to go away.

Which left him no choice.

He would just have to leave. Get them to sign the contract and go home. His time working in the orchard was nearly up. Surely a week or two would make no difference? He'd more than earned his keep.

Besides, the longer he stayed, the more the circumstances that had brought him here niggled at his psyche. It had been easy to come and present a contract to strangers and expect it to be signed, not caring one way or another whether it was the right deal for them or not, but he'd come to like Gus and respect him, and if truth be told, he liked Holly too, maybe a little too much. He didn't like this feeling that he'd come here because he'd had to, not because he'd ever given a damn who'd been awarded the contract.

He looked back at the sleeping woman in his bed, an ache in his chest now, along with his hip. It would end. It would have to. But first they would have tomorrow. It was her day after all, and he'd planned a surprise to take her mind off her nerves.

One more day and one more night.

Then Sunday he'd take her home and tell them both he had to leave. Gus would understand.

And Holly had always known this was temporary.

And one day she would thank him for it.

If it had taken her fifteen minutes to wriggle out of the boa constrictor two days before, it was taking twice that to get into it. Franco wandered out of the bathroom, lazily tying a black bow tie at his neck. 'We've got ten minutes, Holly.' His feet and his hands stopped dead. 'What the hell is that?'

'A body shaper thingy,' she said, feeling yesterday's day spa serenity slipping away, annoyed that he wanted them ready by five when the cocktail party didn't start until six and the Opera House was only a stone's throw away. The hairdresser and make-up artist had taken up the rest of the afternoon since lunch and she would have dearly loved five minutes without people prodding at her to allow her to catch her breath.

'What's it for?'

'So I don't bulge. Bulging is verboten apparently.'

'Take it off.'

'No,' she said, still struggling to get the thing up to her thighs, wondering how she was going to get the rest of herself into it. 'Apparently it does wonders for my figure.'

He put his hand to her arm to stop her struggles. 'You don't need that thing. You don't bulge. Your figure is perfect.'

'But—'

'Perfect, Holly, just the way it is. I know.'

She blinked up at him. 'What if the dress doesn't fit?'

'Of course it will fit. You tried it on before, didn't you?'

'But only with this thing underneath!'

He slapped her on her behind. 'Not a problem. You've always got that gown from Betty's.'

And she slapped him right back. 'You may live to regret saying that.'

The dress fitted perfectly, of course, just as he knew it would. Just like he'd known she would look amazing if she made a little more use of what she had.

But when he'd done the zipper up to the top and she turned to show him, he just hadn't realised how very perfect, how very amazing, she could be.

She was, quite simply, a goddess, her hair tangled into

a sweeping asymmetrical style that balanced the sparkling clasp on her shoulder. Diamond earrings and a shred of sparkle at her wrist were her only other adornment. She didn't need anything more, not with those turquoise eyes and that dress conspiring to bring him undone. He'd always fantasised about peeling her out of a gown that was worthy of her and he wondered how much time they had to spare before the surprise he had planned for her.

A glance at his watch made him frown. Nowhere near enough for what he had planned. Their last night together. Strange, to think that.

But it would be a good one.

Her eyes told him he was taking far too long in putting voice to how he thought she looked and any second now her teeth would be working on those lips that the make-up artist had taken an age to get absolutely perfect and he mustn't ruin, no matter how tempted. He tilted her chin, pressed his lips softly to hers and drew back a little. 'You look beautiful, Holly.' She trembled a little at that, her eyes suddenly wide, afraid. 'You're not worried about tonight, are you?' After a blink of her turquoise eyes she gave a small nod of her head.

'There's no need,' he said. 'Whatever happens tonight, you'll always be a winner.'

Words, she thought as he opened the door to the suite for her. Pretty, empty words. Just like the heated looks from his smoky eyes. Ultimately empty. Devoid of substance.

She knew this for a fact.

She knew it was what she'd agreed to.

And still it was impossible not to wish it was real.

Impossible not to fear that it was already too late...

'Where are we going?' she asked when he led her towards the stairwell rather than the elevator like she'd been expecting.

He smiled enigmatically. 'Wait and see.' He put a hand under her elbow as he guided her carefully up the stairs, her hands busy keeping the hem of her skirt above her toes. He opened the door at the top. 'Your carriage awaits.'

She laughed when she realised what he'd done. Another surprise. 'We're going in that?'

'We are,' he said, taking her arm in his, leading her to the helicopter, 'via the scenic route.'

The smiling pilot organised headsets and Holly was grateful that Franco carefully fitted hers around her hair. And then they were ready and the chopper blades started rotating and her stomach flipped as they lost contact with the building and rose up high, soon soaring over the skyline of one of the most beautiful cities in the world. Somehow Sydney had turned on the perfect day, or maybe Franco had organised that too, the sky a perfect cloudless blue and the sun dancing on the waters of the harbour until it sparkled like the clasp on her dress.

'So this is why we had to be ready so early?' she shouted to Franco.

'Surprised?'

And she was about to nod, but then life had been one surprise after another since Franco had blown into her life such a few short weeks ago. 'Not really,' she said with a shake of her head in case her voice didn't carry, and she squeezed the hand that had taken hers in his as soon as they'd taken off. She wondered how many more surprises he had in store for her, knowing that there was one surprise he wouldn't be springing and she was mad to hope he might.

'Look,' he said, pointing out her window, and there it was, the iconic Sydney Harbour Bridge. They skimmed over the top before turning for another view and then heading along the harbour, past the Opera House on the right where tonight's award ceremony would be held, and out towards the heads.

This was the way to see Sydney, Holly thought, as it was all there, all laid out below them—the beautiful gardens, the tiny bays, the mansions lining the shore and the sandy beaches.

She imagined they'd return to the hotel at the end, but no, the helicopter put down at a helipad adjacent to the Opera House where he handed her out and they dipped low under the blades.

They still had a little time so they stood by the harbour edge awhile, taking in a different view of the harbour, from a different perspective, and Holly knew that even if she didn't win tonight, this day would still remain one of the highlights of her life.

'How was that?' he asked. 'Do you feel better now?'

She looked up at him as he kissed her softly on the mouth and realised that he'd done this all for her, to make her blood fizz with exhilaration instead of fretting with nerves.

And he'd succeeded.

Because the exhilaration was there.

And the nerves were gone.

But she'd been right to fear.

Because as his lips pressed his sweet kiss on her, she realised with heart-thudding certainty that it was already too late.

She'd fallen in love with Franco Chatsfield.

Somehow she made it through the cocktail reception. Somehow she made it through the presentation of the finalists, though she knew her speech thanking Gus had sounded stiff and jerky.

'You're a finalist in one of Australia's most prestigious

wine awards, you're allowed to be nervous,' Franco told her when she rejoined him after her speech. 'But don't worry, you looked so beautiful up there, I don't think anybody noticed. Now relax and have a good time. This is your night, Holly Purman.'

She smiled but how could she relax when she had just made one of life's great discoveries, only to know that she'd made one of life's greatest blunders?

She'd fallen in love with the man she couldn't have.

She was doomed.

She'd never really expected to win. That had allowed her to talk to the people at her table and eat the meal that had been put in front of her even though it might have been made of sawdust.

So when she heard her name it didn't twig, not until the people at her table cheered and Franco had flung his arms around her and the news permeated the fog that was her brain.

'You won, Holly!' Franco said. 'You won!'

And the shock restarted her heart and cleared the fog in her head and she stood on shaky legs to the auditorium's applause, her hand over her mouth, wondering what the hell she was going to say now she'd already thanked Gus. And she found one thing she could say that might not end the pain when Franco left, but it might at least let her cauterise the wound with one last night of pleasure.

Someone was there to hand her up the stairs to the podium and she didn't trip, she didn't fall, she made it there in one piece and received her beautiful award, a stylised golden vine on an earth-brown timber base.

Then it was time to make her acceptance speech.

Franco watched her with a mixture of pride and relief. She deserved the award, she truly did. One part of him was happy for her. But she would be even busier now with interviews and television appearances in the coming weeks as the news of her win got out. It was a good time for him to disappear.

He heard her thank the audience and the Wine Association and give thanks to Gus once again for teaching her everything she knew.

He heard her pay tribute to her fellow finalists, all of whom were worthy winners.

And then she paused, and like everyone else in the room Franco waited, and saw her eyes find him in the crowd. She hugged the award to her chest. 'This is turning out to be quite some year,' she started. 'A few weeks ago Purman Wines had an offer some might say was too good to refuse.'

Franco's legs pushed him up higher in his seat.

'So, naturally, I turned it down.'

The audience laughed. All except Franco, who wondered what was coming, every part of him on tenterhooks.

'Luckily for us, the person making the offer was insistent and wouldn't go away. Luckily for us, he stuck around. It's too early just yet to give details of this offer, but it's a very good deal and we will be signing with this group this coming week, probably as soon as I get home, so you'll hear about it very soon.'

Yes! It was perfect. He'd have the deal and there would be no reason for him to stay any longer.

She was smiling at him now and he was smiling right back.

'I'd like to thank this person for his offer and for his refusal to go home when I demanded it—' more laughter here '—but most of all I'd like to thank him for his faith in our wines and his determination to acquire them, because ultimately, what better compliment can a winemaker ask?'

Her words grated deep into his senses, the euphoria

he'd felt just a moment ago already slipping away in the wounds.

Faith in her wines?

Determination to have them?

Yes to the second. But the second was in no way related to the first. The second had far more to do with another motivation that had nothing to do with her wines. They could have tasted like home brew, for all he cared, and still he would have signed them up, because that's what Christos wanted if Franco was to be assured the cash flow from the Chatsfield Family Trust. And so that's what Christos would get.

Up on the podium, Holly nestled the award alongside her shoulder. 'I hope this award tonight goes some way to vindicate that faith and resolve to have Purman Wines served at his tables. Thank you.'

Franco felt sick to the core.

She left the podium to a standing ovation. People at the table were pumping his hand, conversation was buzzing with speculation, and all he wanted to do was disappear. Hide. Vanish. He'd been here under false pretences the entire time. And there was no time to process that because Holly was back and he had to perform, to do the right thing, so he folded her in his arms and kissed her cheek and congratulated her. He didn't know whether the resistance he felt in her body was due to some failure in his efforts or because she was still buzzing from the win or something else.

It was hours before they made it back to the hotel but it was still not long enough for Franco's liking. There'd been congratulatory drinks and then an afterparty hosted by a nearby wine bar and all the time he'd dreaded being back in the suite, to the tatters of the night he'd had planned.

And all the time the guilt had weighed down on him, like a weight dropped from a great height upon his chest. It had been too easy, he realised, too easy all along. He'd had the Purmans' agreement in his pocket weeks ago, all he had to do was the time, and the cash flow from the Chatsfield Family Trust would be his.

But since that first day when she'd accused him of being a messenger boy, he'd never considered how Holly saw his part in this deal. He'd worked in the vineyard to prove he was the kind of person they could do business with. The kind of person they could trust.

But it had always been about the money.

Nothing had changed since then.

It was still all about the money.

And he was still a messenger boy.

And he hated himself for it.

CHAPTER THIRTEEN

'I CAN'T BELIEVE it,' Holly said as she put the award down in the centre of the dining table and admired it some more. 'I still can't believe I won. I may have to take this to bed with me. I hope you don't mind.'

Franco didn't mind. He figured she might as well sleep with something. It sure as hell wouldn't be him.

It couldn't be him. Not now.

'You deserve it, Holly.' He could say that honestly, even if his voice, like his spirit, was flat.

'And Gus was just so excited when I rang and told him.' She looked at him and smiled and for the first time he noticed the tautness around her eyes and the tension around her mouth.

'He must be very proud.'

'He is.' A pause, and then, 'You haven't mentioned my speech at all.'

Ah. There was good reason for that. 'It was a good speech,' he conceded. 'People laughed. You did well.'

'And? I thought you'd be a bit more excited. You'll have your contract signed. You'll be free to go home like you always wanted.'

He looked at her. It might have been the end of a long night filled with celebration and her hair and make-up might be a little less perfect than when she started, but yet she was still utterly gorgeous.

It struck him then what he was giving up when he left. He was going to lose Holly from his life. Forever. And his gut twisted at the notion of never seeing her again. But what right did he have to want for anything else?

What right did he have to hope for anything else?

None at all.

Holly stepped closer to him, took one of his hands and placed it against one perfect breast. 'So, don't you want to celebrate? While you're still here? While you still can.'

In spite of himself, his fingers squeezed, and he closed his eyes and ached to do more. It would be so easy to do more, so easy to blot it all out and lose himself in pleasure, but he was already living a lie, and at some stage the lies had to stop.

It was time for the pretence to stop.

He opened his eyes to see tears in hers and he ached for all the hurt and he knew this couldn't go on.

'Forget the contract,' he said.

'What?'

'Tear it up. Throw it on the fire. I don't care. Just don't sign it.'

She shook her head. 'I don't understand.'

'Don't sign it. Because your speech was good,' he said, pulling his hand from her, 'but it was flawed.'

She blinked up at him. 'Why?'

'Because you credited me with too much. Because I never came here because I had faith in Purman Wines. I never stayed because I had faith in Purman Wines.'

Her eyes were wide with confusion. 'What?'

'I came here for money. Purely and simply for money. Because if I didn't get your signature on the dotted line, I'd be cut off for ever from the cash flow from the Chatsfield Family Trust and I couldn't afford to lose it. So I had no choice. I had to get you to sign.'

Her hands were in her hair, her nails pressing into her scalp. She could not be hearing this. 'What are you saying?'

'I did it for the money, Holly. I only ever did it for the money. I came here wanting your signature so that I could keep my share of the Chatsfield empire's income.'

It made no sense to Holly. She'd thought that her declaration of the impending contract would put a full stop on their relationship, but not now, just in a day or two, when the contract was signed. And until then, she'd still have those days and nights.

But now? He was telling her he'd never been interested in their wines, just the signature on a contract...

And the gears and cogs of her mind turned back a few short weeks and she remembered a man who had come here in one God-awful hurry, and not been interested in the vineyard or the winery or the cellar door or anything more than getting their signature on the dotted line.

'You never did care about any of it,' she said, thinking back as all the pieces fell into place. 'You didn't even want to taste our wine. And that's why. Because it didn't matter to you.' She looked up at him then and asked him how much. He named an annual figure and she closed her eyes again.

She should be flattered, she guessed. That was one almighty signing fee.

And not the only fee he'd extracted from this deal.

Oh, God, she was all kinds of stupid. She'd offered herself to him on a silver platter.

How old did you have to be before you learned when you were being played? How many times did you have to fall for the worst kind of man—the one who said pretty words and sounded like he meant them when all the time he was just stringing you along?

'So what was I?' she demanded, her voice becoming shrill and there was no way she could prevent it. 'The bonus?'

'Holly, that had nothing to do with it.'

'Really? Because that's how it looks to me, Franco. That's very much how it looks to me. You get a gold-plated deal and a lovely commission and take whatever you can get on the side.'

'You offered! You practically begged me to make love to you! To help you out with your little problem. Don't you remember?'

She shrugged his words away. Nothing he could say could make up for what he had done. 'What kind of low-life are you? We trusted you, Gus and me, and you reward that trust by treating us like some kind of keys to your fortune?'

'Then don't sign!' he said. 'I don't want you to sign. Forget I was ever here.'

'I'll forget you ever lived, Franco Chatsfield!' she cried as the best day of her life rapidly turned into the worst. 'Just go!'

CHAPTER FOURTEEN

WINTER MOVED INTO spring. The days grew slowly warmer and sunnier. There was always something to do, always work in the vineyard or the cellar door or even about the house, and yet for Holly, day dragged wearily after day. Even bud burst, usually her favourite time of year as the vines burst back into life, failed to lift her spirits.

Gus did his best to cheer her up, she knew, and she loved him for it. But she didn't have the heart to laugh at his stories any more. She tried to, she really did, but she just didn't have the heart for anything. Somebody else had ripped her heart away.

Franco.

'You'll be all right,' Gus encouraged her one evening as she picked at her food. 'You'll get over him. He wasn't good enough for you, just like that other bloke.'

And she smiled at her grandfather and nodded, because she loved him, but Franco hadn't been like that other bloke at all. She'd never loved Mark Turner, she'd known that for years now. She'd been young and flattered and in love with the idea of being in love, and then she'd been devastated when he'd turned around and walked away and done all he could to trash their brand into the deal. So hurt that she'd turned her hurt into anger and blamed it all on the grandfather who had done her such a big favour by getting rid of him.

There was no comparison between the two.

Loving Franco had shown her what love was. And loving Franco had shown her what it really felt like to experience deep, gut-wrenching hurt.

So she smiled for her grandfather and did what she had to do in the vineyard, while inside she grieved for what she had lost.

Then one night she needed to look something up and was searching for a book on winemaking in the study when she came across the wrapped-up package that Franco had left behind when he'd thrown his clothes into a bag in a Sydney hotel room, and disappeared from her life. She'd put it in her luggage and brought it home, meaning to send it on.

She forgot about the book as she looked at the wrapping. It was just a photograph—it wouldn't hurt to have a look, she reasoned. They'd been there together that day after all. She slipped a nail under the tape and eased it off, unwrapping the paper from the frame.

The mother koala looked into the lens, inquisitive but not bothered, a twig of gum leaves clutched in one paw, while the joey nestled against her chest. But it was the words engraved on the gold plate underneath that drew her eye, words written in both Italian and English.

For Nikki's Ward,
dedicated to the memory of Nikki.

And then a date.

Curious, she went to her computer and searched and found and read a webpage about a hospital in Italy with a ward for children with kidney disease, Nikki's Ward, that was funded entirely by one Franco Chatsfield.

There was a picture of a little girl with large, grey eyes and wavy long sandy hair, and a vice clamped hard around her heart because she didn't have to read any more to know whose child she was.

Franco's child.

He hadn't given up his kidney for his friend. It had been to save his own daughter's life. Except it hadn't.

And she thought about the scar at his side and how much it must cost to run a ward for children with kidney disease, and her heart ached for a man with secrets.

A man she would never see again.

He was helping with the harvest when he heard the news. He'd returned to Italy and thrown himself into work, but he couldn't sit still in his office for five minutes, he couldn't focus. So he helped out with the harvest instead. He picked the grapes that had rescued him once before, when he was just a teenager running away from a family he thought didn't want him and where he could never see himself belonging.

And one day, after a day's picking, he'd returned to his office and found an email from Christos Giatrakos waiting for him, an email he'd almost deleted, until he'd registered the subject line.

From: Christos.Giatrakos@TheChatsfield.com
To: Franco.Chatsfield@TheChatsfield.com
Subject: CONGRATULATIONS
Purman Wines has signed and returned their contract with the Chatsfields. As per our agreement, your entitlements under the Chatsfield Family Trust will continue.

I would also like to extend an invitation to the share-
holders' meeting in August. More info to follow.
C.G.

Franco could barely believe the words. He'd sat and
stared a long time at that email.

And he'd wondered about a woman who was full of
surprises.

And who'd just given him the biggest surprise of them
all.

The cellar door had been busy with a couple of last-minute
bus tours and Holly had sent Josh home before finishing
the dishes and hanging up the last few glasses in the racks
herself. Josh had a date with Rachel from the bakery again
and she was happy for him, even though he'd looked guilty
about going out to have fun and leaving her finishing up.

She didn't mind. Sooner or later she'd get over Franco,
and until then, she might as well stay busy. That was the
good thing about working in a vineyard and winery—
there was always something to do, even if it couldn't stop
her thinking.

Did Franco ever stop to think about her? Probably not.
He was probably relieved to have escaped at last, back to
his own vines in Italy where the women no doubt looked
like women. Did he have a woman now?

She shook her head as she racked the last glass and
gave the bench top a final wipe down. Sometimes it didn't
pay to think.

She heard the crunch of gravel and the growl of an en-
gine outside and cursed herself for worrying about the
dishes before bringing in the open sign. She glanced out
the window, seeing the bonnet of a flashy red car pulled up
outside. Typical, she thought, someone down from the big

smoke trying to cram in as many wineries as they could for the day. She was glad she'd sent Josh home because he would have stayed for the duration, whereas she wasn't in the mood to be hospitable.

'I'm sorry, we're actually closed,' she said, busy wiping down the sink as the door swung open behind her. There was no time to waste on pleasantries.

'I'm not here to taste.'

Her hands stilled on the sink's edge and she used them to hold herself up.

She spun around and found Franco standing in the doorway, larger than life, his chiselled Chatsfield good looks even more beautiful than she remembered.

'I called by the house. Gus said you were here. He's walking. He looks good.'

And a shiver ran down her spine. She knew he hadn't come to see how Gus was. 'Is there a problem with the wine?' They'd recently sent a batch of the sparkling Rubida to London for Gene Chatsfield's upcoming wedding. 'If anything's happened...'

He shook his head. 'It's good. All good.' But then he frowned. 'What happened to the khaki uniform?'

Holly glanced down at her fitted floral dress—the result of a spontaneous shopping trip to Adelaide the day she'd gone to disgorge and dosage the order for Gene's wedding. Because after working there alone, in that space, after the day she'd spent working there with Franco, she'd needed cheering up. She'd spent a lot of money in her effort to cheer up and it had worked too, for all of five minutes.

But the dress had become one of her spring favourites with its square neck and cap sleeves and it made her feel good wearing it.

'I save that for when I'm working in the vineyard.'

He nodded, approval in his eyes. 'You look good.'

So do you. 'Thank you.'

He just continued to stare at her with those grey eyes and she let him because it gave her an excuse to stare right back at him. How many nights had she lain awake thinking of Franco? Remembering Franco? Picturing him in her mind's eye? And yet her memories had done the man an injustice. He was taller somehow, his shoulders broader, his features more chiselled, his olive skin darker, like he'd spent time working outside under a Piacenzan sun.

He was so beautiful it ached to look at him, knowing she'd been in his orbit for a time—such a short time— until their paths had spun them apart in different directions and she'd lost him.

It hurt even more to feel the tiny flicker of hope that curled from her heart, knowing how likely and how easily it would be extinguished. She forced herself not to let it catch.

'So…why are you here?'

He blinked like he'd lost his way and had to find his way back.

'Why did you sign?'

A nerve twitched in her cheek. She squared her shoulders, strangely disappointed. 'It's a good deal. Too good to turn down. Already Chatsfield's is apparently working on a new marketing campaign featuring the new menus and wine choices. It's all good.'

'You didn't have to sign.'

'I know. I didn't do it for you.' She hadn't done it for Nikki's Ward either—in spite of what had happened, Gus and Holly had signed the week after she'd won the award and she hadn't known about Nikki's Ward then.

He turned and raked a hand through his hair and it was killing her to see him looking so tortured but she had her own pain to deal with. She couldn't take his on too. Not if all he was bringing was more pain. Not if this tiny flicker of hope so valiantly persisting in her chest was only going to be quashed. She crossed her arms to protect the feeble flame.

'So if that's all? Because we're closed.'

He took a wavering step closer. 'Holly, when I left, I left something behind.'

The picture. Nikki's picture.

And she had to close her eyes as that flicker of hope fizzled into nothingness.

'I'm sorry, Franco. You didn't have to come all this way. I was going to post the photo. I just hadn't—' *been able to bring myself to do it* '—got around to it.'

'Thank you,' he said. 'But I'm not here for the photograph. But first, I have to explain something.'

Her heart skipped a beat. But she had something to tell him too. 'I know about Nikki's Ward.'

'You do? But—'

'The photo. I opened it. I saw the plaque. I looked up Nikki's Ward on the computer—it wasn't hard. You founded that ward, Franco, and you fund it. I don't know how much it would cost to run, but I'm guessing you rely on those distributions from the Chatsfield Family Trust. And that's why you needed that contract signed. That's why you were so determined to stay until you had secured it. Am I warm?'

His grey eyes surveyed her, and he gave the merest dip of his head in acknowledgement.

'Nikki was your daughter. She was the one you donated your kidney to.'

He shook his head and looked at the floor, and when he raised his head again he smiled softly. 'I never even knew I had a daughter until she was five. I probably would never have known—except she was sick and her mother came looking for me. The only hope was to find a match for a kidney transplant. I was her best chance and I was that match.'

Oh, Franco. And her heart went out to him, because she knew how this story ended, and she knew what it was costing him to even talk about it, but she didn't move an inch. Didn't budge. Because this was his story and he had to tell it.

'There was a window of hope, where we thought that she would be okay, but eventually her little body rejected it, and she caught infection after infection and withered slowly away before our eyes. I watched her die, and as she died, I promised myself I would never expose myself to hurt like that again.'

She ached to hold him, to comfort him, but she dared not move. How could she move, when there was an ocean of pain to navigate between them?

'Michele—her mother—and I broke up after that. There was too much pressure. Too much need. She was desperate for another child.' He looked away. 'But it wasn't the same. We'd got back together for Nikki's sake, but without Nikki...' His voice cracked. 'I just couldn't go there.'

'She was the one,' she said, understanding. 'The one you judged me against.'

'Unfairly,' he said, his grey eyes on her. 'I know it was unfair. You were never anything like her. It took losing you to make me realise that.'

Her heart skipped a beat.

'Why?'

'Because when she left, I felt relief, like there was a chance for me to believe I might one day live again, however long it took. But when I left you...'

She didn't dare breathe. 'What?'

'It felt like my heart had been ripped from my chest—

a heart I didn't realise I had. I was numb all over again. Except this time, I'd brought it on myself.'

She felt herself sway on the spot, her own heart thudding so hard and fast in her chest that she had to put a hand over it to stop it jumping right out. This was the moment she'd dreamed of so many times since he'd left, so surely she must be dreaming. But when she blinked and opened her eyes, he was still standing there across the room from her, and the hand over her chest felt hope dance inside.

'I can't imagine what it must be like,' she said, 'to lose a child.'

He smiled a sad smile. 'When Nikki died, it killed something inside me. I'd known her such a short time. An intense time. And after she died, there was simply nothing left of a heart that had been shattered into a million pieces, that I was sure could never be repaired. I knew I could never love again.'

He paused, baring his teeth, his lips pulled back tight as he breathed, as if it hurt. 'I was wrong.'

Part of her wanted to hope and dream he had come back for her and to throw herself into his arms, but she'd been in those arms before, only to have them push her away and that had been such a terrible thing. And she was still so very, very raw and she wasn't sure she could endure it if it happened a second time. So instead she mustered every remaining shred of strength she could find, and asked, 'What changed your mind?'

He looked at her with those storm-tossed grey eyes and said, 'You did.'

Sensation zippered down her spine as the air was sucked from her lungs.

'How?' she whispered.

'I'm not sure. But when I went back to Italy, I couldn't settle at my desk. So I worked with the pickers on the harvest. We sat together for lunch in the shade of the vines. We talked and laughed and ate together, and that was better and I told myself I was happier, but still there was this heaviness in my chest that would not go away.

'I thought it was emptiness, because my kidney scar aches and my kidney is gone. I convinced myself it was emptiness because I didn't want to find another explanation.

'Except that didn't explain why it hurt more when I thought of you. If there was no heart, if I was just empty, I should feel nothing. And so I tried to put you out of my mind. I tried to forget, but there was no putting you out of my mind, just as there was no forgetting, and every time I thought of you, it hurt more and more.

'Then I realised it hurt because my heart was there. Because, slowly and inexorably, you had put the pieces of my heart back together.'

He looked at her and shrugged. 'And I don't even know how it happened. I told myself you weren't my type and still I wanted you. I warned you not to be needy but if anyone is needy here it's me. I needed you so much I had to come back, to find out if you could ever forgive me for what I did. To find out if you might feel a fraction of what I do.'

Could a heart possibly thud any louder?

'What do you feel?'

'Empty without you. Because I need you by my side. I need you in my bed. I want you for my wife. And all because I love you, Holly. I want to be whole again and I cannot see how I can be whole without you, without a lifetime of you by my side.'

The silence weighed heavily between them, while the ocean between them leached away and let her pass, until she was in his arms, her arms around his neck, his around her as he whirled her into a kiss, their first kiss as more than mere lovers. Their first kiss as a couple in love.

She let that kiss speak for her and wipe away the hurt and the pain, let that kiss show him her love and her hopes and her dreams she hadn't dare dream.

Until this very moment.

When finally they stopped to draw breath, and to smile at each other and to laugh and kiss again, she put her hands to the beautiful face of the man she loved and found the words she needed to say. 'I love you, Franco Chatsfield. And a lifetime spent with you sounds just about perfect.'

And it was.

* * * * *

If you enjoyed this book, look out for the next instalment of THE CHATSFIELD:
*RIVAL'S CHALLENGE by Abby Green,
coming next month.*

Mills & Boon® Hardback
September 2014

ROMANCE

The Housekeeper's Awakening	Sharon Kendrick
More Precious than a Crown	Carol Marinelli
Captured by the Sheikh	Kate Hewitt
A Night in the Prince's Bed	Chantelle Shaw
Damaso Claims His Heir	Annie West
Changing Constantinou's Game	Jennifer Hayward
The Ultimate Revenge	Victoria Parker
Tycoon's Temptation	Trish Morey
The Party Dare	Anne Oliver
Sleeping with the Soldier	Charlotte Phillips
All's Fair in Lust & War	Amber Page
Dressed to Thrill	Bella Frances
Interview with a Tycoon	Cara Colter
Her Boss by Arrangement	Teresa Carpenter
In Her Rival's Arms	Alison Roberts
Frozen Heart, Melting Kiss	Ellie Darkins
After One Forbidden Night...	Amber McKenzie
Dr Perfect on Her Doorstep	Lucy Clark

MEDICAL

A Secret Shared...	Marion Lennox
Flirting with the Doc of Her Dreams	Janice Lynn
The Doctor Who Made Her Love Again	Susan Carlisle
The Maverick Who Ruled Her Heart	Susan Carlisle

0814GEN STD HB

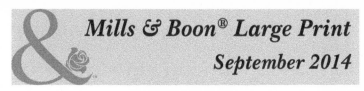

Mills & Boon® Large Print

September 2014

ROMANCE

The Only Woman to Defy Him	Carol Marinelli
Secrets of a Ruthless Tycoon	Cathy Williams
Gambling with the Crown	Lynn Raye Harris
The Forbidden Touch of Sanguardo	Julia James
One Night to Risk it All	Maisey Yates
A Clash with Cannavaro	Elizabeth Power
The Truth About De Campo	Jennifer Hayward
Expecting the Prince's Baby	Rebecca Winters
The Millionaire's Homecoming	Cara Colter
The Heir of the Castle	Scarlet Wilson
Twelve Hours of Temptation	Shoma Narayanan

HISTORICAL

Unwed and Unrepentant	Marguerite Kaye
Return of the Prodigal Gilvry	Ann Lethbridge
A Traitor's Touch	Helen Dickson
Yield to the Highlander	Terri Brisbin
Return of the Viking Warrior	Michelle Styles

MEDICAL

Waves of Temptation	Marion Lennox
Risk of a Lifetime	Caroline Anderson
To Play with Fire	Tina Beckett
The Dangers of Dating Dr Carvalho	Tina Beckett
Uncovering Her Secrets	Amalie Berlin
Unlocking the Doctor's Heart	Susanne Hampton

Mills & Boon® Hardback

October 2014

ROMANCE

An Heiress for His Empire	Lucy Monroe
His for a Price	Caitlin Crews
Commanded by the Sheikh	Kate Hewitt
The Valquez Bride	Melanie Milburne
The Uncompromising Italian	Cathy Williams
Prince Hafiz's Only Vice	Susanna Carr
A Deal Before the Altar	Rachael Thomas
Rival's Challenge	Abby Green
The Party Starts at Midnight	Lucy King
Your Bed or Mine?	Joss Wood
Turning the Good Girl Bad	Avril Tremayne
Breaking the Bro Code	Stefanie London
The Billionaire in Disguise	Soraya Lane
The Unexpected Honeymoon	Barbara Wallace
A Princess by Christmas	Jennifer Faye
His Reluctant Cinderella	Jessica Gilmore
One More Night with Her Desert Prince...	Jennifer Taylor
From Fling to Forever	Avril Tremayne

MEDICAL

It Started with No Strings...	Kate Hardy
Flirting with Dr Off-Limits	Robin Gianna
Dare She Date Again?	Amy Ruttan
The Surgeon's Christmas Wish	Annie O'Neil

0914GEN STD HB

Mills & Boon® Large Print

October 2014

ROMANCE

Ravelli's Defiant Bride	Lynne Graham
When Da Silva Breaks the Rules	Abby Green
The Heartbreaker Prince	Kim Lawrence
The Man She Can't Forget	Maggie Cox
A Question of Honour	Kate Walker
What the Greek Can't Resist	Maya Blake
An Heir to Bind Them	Dani Collins
Becoming the Prince's Wife	Rebecca Winters
Nine Months to Change His Life	Marion Lennox
Taming Her Italian Boss	Fiona Harper
Summer with the Millionaire	Jessica Gilmore

HISTORICAL

Scars of Betrayal	Sophia James
Scandal's Virgin	Louise Allen
An Ideal Companion	Anne Ashley
Surrender to the Viking	Joanna Fulford
No Place for an Angel	Gail Whitiker

MEDICAL

200 Harley Street: Surgeon in a Tux	Carol Marinelli
200 Harley Street: Girl from the Red Carpet	Scarlet Wilson
Flirting with the Socialite Doc	Melanie Milburne
His Diamond Like No Other	Lucy Clark
The Last Temptation of Dr Dalton	Robin Gianna
Resisting Her Rebel Hero	Lucy Ryder

MILLS & BOON®

Why shop at millsandboon.co.uk?

Each year, thousands of romance readers find their perfect read at millsandboon.co.uk. That's because we're passionate about bringing you the very best romantic fiction. Here are some of the advantages of shopping at www.millsandboon.co.uk:

* **Get new books first**—you'll be able to buy your favourite books one month before they hit the shops

* **Get exclusive discounts**—you'll also be able to buy our specially created monthly collections, with up to 50% off the RRP

* **Find your favourite authors**—latest news, interviews and new releases for all your favourite authors and series on our website, plus ideas for what to try next

* **Join in**—once you've bought your favourite books, don't forget to register with us to rate, review and join in the discussions

Visit **www.millsandboon.co.uk**
for all this and more today!